Ox-Tales
FIRE

*Original stories from
remarkable writers*

Ox-Tales are published in support of

 Oxfam

First published in Great Britain in 2009 by *Green*Profile, an imprint of
Profile Books Ltd, 3A Exmouth House, Pine Street, London EC1R 0JH

Printed in the UK by CPI Bookmarque, Croydon, CR0 4TD
Typeset in Iowan to a design by Sue Lamble

1 3 5 7 9 10 8 6 4 2

A CIP catalogue record for this book is
available from the British Library
ISBN: 978 1 84668 259 9

Mixed Sources
Product group from well-managed
forests and other controlled sources
www.fsc.org   Cert no. TT-COC-002227
© 1996 Forest Stewardship Council

Ox-Tales: Fire

OX-TALES: FIRE is one of four original collections, featuring stories by leading British- and Irish-based writers. Each of the writers has contributed their story for free in order to raise money and awareness for Oxfam. The FOUR ELEMENTS provide a loose framework for the stories and highlight key areas of Oxfam's work: water projects (WATER), aid for conflict areas (FIRE), agricultural development (EARTH), and action on climate change (AIR). An afterword, at the end of each book, explains how Oxfam makes a difference. And in buying this book, you'll be a part of that process, too.

Compiling these books, we asked authors for new stories; or, from novelists who don't do short stories, work in progress from their next book. The response was thirty-eight original pieces of fiction, which are spread across the four books and framed by a cycle of element poems by Vikram Seth. We think they're extraordinary, but be your own judge. And if you like what you read here, please buy all four OX-TALES books – and help Oxfam work towards an end to poverty worldwide.

Mark Ellingham (Profile) & Peter Florence (Hay Festival),
Editors, OX-TALES

Acknowledgments

The Ox-Tales books were developed at Profile Books by Mark Ellingham in association with Peter Florence and Hay Festival. Thanks from us both to the authors who contributed stories – and time – to creating these four collections in support of Oxfam. And thanks, too, to their publishers and agents who, without exception, offered generous support to this project.

At Oxfam, Tom Childs has guided the project alongside Suzy Smith, Charlie Hayes, Annie Lewis, Fee Gilfeather, Annemarie Papatheofilou and Matt Kurton.

At Profile, Peter Dyer, Penny Daniel, Niamh Murray, Duncan Clark, Claire Beaumont, Simon Shelmerdine, Ruth Killick, Rebecca Gray, Kate Griffin and Andrew Franklin have been instrumental. Thanks also to Nikky Twyman and Caroline Pretty for proofreading, and to Jonathan Gray for his cover illustrations.

Contents

VIKRAM SETH (born Calcutta, India, 1952) is the author of the novels *The Golden Gate* (1986), *A Suitable Boy* (1993) and *An Equal Music* (1999), and of books of poetry, travel, fable and memoir.

'Fire' is part of a sequence of poems, *Seven Elements*, incorporating the elements in the European, Indian and Chinese traditions (earth, air, fire, water, wood, metal and space). Set to music by the composer Alec Roth, *Seven Elements* will be performed in summer 2009 at the Salisbury, Chelsea and Lichfield festivals.

Fire

Fa-yaah
O fayah – fayah – fayaaah
Dizayaah
Hot hot hot
I'm burning a lot with dizayaah
O fayah fayah fayah
Hot as a filament wa-yah
Hot as prawn jamba-la-yah
I'm burning so hot
I'm baking a pot –
O hot hot hot as dizayaah
Fa-yaah! Fa-yaah!

All was born from me –
All your eyes can see.
Who gave life and birth
To sun and star and earth?
Who gave pulse and germ
To man and beast and worm?
Who is hot hot hot
When black space is not?
Who is bright bright bright
In this endless night?
Fa-yaah! Fa-yaah! Fa-yaah!

Fa-yaah
O fayah – fayah – fayaaah
Dizayaah
Hot hot hot
I'm burning a lot with dizayaah
O fayah fayah fayah
Hot as a funeral pa-yaah
Leaping up ha-yaah and ha-yaah –
I sizzle, I daze,
I fizzle, I blaze,
I scorch, I toast,
I smoulder, I roast,
I flare, I excite,
I flash, I ignite,
I rage, I lust,
I blaze, I combust,
Red, yellow, white,
I light up the night,
This endless night, with dizayaah,
O fa-yaah! Fa-yaah! Fa-yaah!

Vikram Seth

The Island

MARK HADDON (born Northampton, 1962) is an author, illustrator and screenwriter who has written fifteen books for children and won two BAFTAs. His bestselling novel, *The Curious Incident of the Dog in the Night-time* (2003), written for children and adults alike, won seventeen literary prizes, including the Whitbread Award. His second novel, *A Spot of Bother*, was published in 2006. He lives in Oxford with his wife and their two young sons.

SHE'S DREAMING OF THE PINES outside her window in the palace. The way the night wind turns them into a black sea that tumbles and breaks against the stone wall below the sill. She's dreaming of the summer sound of trees being felled further up the mountain, the hollow *tock, tock, tock* of the axe, the slow cracking of the trunk and that final thump. All that splintered yellow, still damp with life. The smell of fresh resin in the air and columns of midges rising and falling in the angled sunlight.

She's dreaming of the wood being split and planed and toothed home into a curved keel that will cut an ocean in half. She's dreaming of this morning, standing on the prow with her husband-to-be, the oars churning the waves to foam and the fat sails slapping in the wind. Over the horizon his city where they'll marry. Behind them the home she'll never see again.

She's dreaming of the wedding, flames dancing in the sconces of a great hall. Flames multiplied in a hundred golden cups. Painted plates heavy with roast meats and chickpeas, quinces and saffron and honey cakes.

She's dreaming of the bridal suite, a snowfall of Egyptian cotton on the bed. Hanging above the pillows is a tapestry, the work so fine she could be looking through a window. In the centre of the picture is a woman weeping on a beach and, far out, in the chop and glitter of the woven sea, a single ship sailing steadily towards the border and the world beyond.

She moves a little closer so that she can see the woman's face, and then it hits her like a punch. She's looking at herself.

She comes round like a drowning woman breaking the water's surface, thrashing and grasping for air. The light hurts her eyes, her throat is dry and the world is foggy from drink, or drugs, or fever.

She rolls over and finds herself in an empty bed. He must be awake and making preparations for today's journey. She stands with some difficulty and realises that she can hear nothing except the cry of gulls and guy ropes humming in the wind.

She staggers to the door, uncouples the four leather straps which bind the canvas flaps and steps outside to find herself in a ghost camp, five squares of flattened, yellow grass, fishbones, a single sandal, the torched circle of last night's fire and, far out, in the chop and glitter of the sea, a single ship.

She tries to scream but there is a weight on her chest that stops her filling her lungs. Her mind bucks and twists, searching for ways to make this right. He's coming back. The crew have mutinied and kidnapped him. Or left him somewhere nearby, tied up, beaten, dead. Then she looks down and sees, beside her feet, a jug of water and a loaf of bread, and on the loaf is the ring she gave him as a sign of their eternal love. And then she knows that he has abandoned her.

The sky revolves, she vomits on the wet grass and the world goes dark.

When time begins again she's skidding down the scree on bloody hands and knees towards the beach, then stumbling over the slip and clack of pebbles to the surf. She yells into the wind and her cry echoes round the rocky cove. Her heart thrashes like a netted bird.

The boat shrinks. She has become the woman in the tapestry.

He is the only man she's ever loved. And he has dumped her like ballast. She needs to find an explanation that does not make her a fool and him an animal, but every thought of him is like a knife turning in the wound love made. She wants to hurl a stack of figured bowls across a room. She wants to weep till someone comes to comfort her. She wants to find a man who'll track him down and slit his throat, or make him realise he's wrong and bring him back.

She turns to take it in, this godforsaken place, bracken and sea-pink, rye grass jerking in the wind, slabs of basalt rusty with lichen. Lying in a shallow pool, she sees the bloody head of a seal pup hacked off by the men last night, then hurled off the cliff before they cooked the body. Its blind eyes have turned white.

She crouches on the hard, wet stones and hugs herself. No-one has any idea that she is here except the crew of the departing ship, and no-one else would give a damn. She does not know the name of this island. She knows only that this is the place in which she will die. She is off the heart's map and her compass is spinning. There are no landmarks. She does not understand the language spoken here.

Minutes pass. Water breaks and fizzes on the pebbles. The wind sings and the cold begins to bite. She stands and starts the long climb to the bed they will never share again.

She is a princess. In twenty years she has never been alone, never cooked a meal, never cleaned a floor. She has bathed in clean, warm water every morning. Twice a day newly laundered clothes have been laid on her bed. She realises that this will be hard. She does not know the meaning of the word.

She enters the tent and sees his body's imprint on the sheets and has to turn away. She eats the bread and drinks the water, then lies down and waits to die, as if an easy death is one more luxury some nameless servant will provide.

She cannot believe that anyone is able to bear this kind of pain. She thinks of shepherds sleepless in the blue snow, their furs pulled tight around their shoulders, waiting for the wolves, armed only with a slingshot. She thinks of the soldiers who come back from every summer's campaign with legs and arms missing, the stumps like melted wax. She thinks of women giving birth in stone sheds with leaking roofs and mud floors. She thinks about what it must take to lead such lives, and she starts to understand that wealth has deprived her of the one skill that she needs now.

The light begins to die and the dark thickens slowly to a colour she has never seen before, like the black inside a stone.

Then the shearwaters come, two hundred thousand birds returning from a day at sea to run the gauntlet of the black-backed gulls, and suddenly the tent is at the centre of a hurricane of screams, the noise that makes young sailors think that they have drifted near the mouth of hell.

She dares not go outside for fear of what she might find. She covers her ears and curls into a ball in the centre of the single rug and waits for claws and teeth to tear the flimsy canvas walls and shred her body like a deer's. She waits, and waits, and when the silence finally comes it is worse, for she has been stripped of everything that used to shield her from this hard world where every action has a consequence. She has no-one else to blame. This is her punishment. She helped him kill her brother. Now she has to die. And when her bones are picked clean, the scales will be level once again.

She should have listened to her maids and walked around the palace grounds, but she had walked around the palace grounds a thousand times. She knew in tedious detail every carved fountain, every lavender bush with its halo of bees, every shaded bower. She wanted the bustle of the quays, those overflowing baskets of squid and mackerel, the stacked crates and coiled ropes, the shouting and the knock of tarred hulls, that childhood fantasy of walking up a gangplank

and casting off and slipping through the cupped hands of
the breakwater into the white light of a world outside her
family's orbit.

They came at every summer's end, a war-price Athens paid
to keep the peace, just one more ceremony in a calendar of
ceremonies, the Leaping of the Bulls, the Festival of Poppies.
Twelve young men and women taken from their ship and
housed in the barn above the orchard, while this year's pit
was dug beside the last, then led out and lined up to have
their throats slit and to die on top of one another. They
were foreigners, human cattle, and they knew this, shuffling
with heads down, already half dead. She gave them no more
thought than she gave the enemies her father and brothers
killed in battle.

But in that moment she saw the one man who held his
head high. His green eyes locked with hers for a second,
maybe two, then he was pushed forward by one of the
guards and she realised that there were many worlds beyond
this world and her own was very small indeed.

Later that night she woke repeatedly, thinking he was
standing in the room, or lying beside her. She was terrified
at first, then disappointed. She felt alive in a way that she
had never felt alive before. The cold flags on the floor, the

cicadas, the pocked coin of the moon, her own skin ... she had never seen or felt these things clearly until now.

Shortly after dawn she slipped past the maids in the outer room and walked round the orchard to the barn. She told the guards she wanted to talk with the prisoners and they could think of no adequate reply to this unexpected request.

The last of the night was pooling in the big stone rooms, the window slits no wider than a hand. There was sand on the floor and the sound of breathing. She felt the stir her presence caused, warm bodies shifting nervously in the dark. It was a small thing to be brave about, but she had never needed to be brave before, and mastering her fear was thrilling.

His face materialised behind the bars of the little window. 'You came.'

She had spent her whole life waiting for this moment and never realised it. She thought stories only happened to men. Now her own story was beginning. She was no longer waiting to hear about other people's adventures.

'My father is the king,' he said. 'In time I will become king. If you save us, I will make you my queen.'

She gave him her ring and he told her what to do. She slid her hand between the bars and let him grip her wrists. She called for help. The guard came running and reached through to free her. The prince wrapped one hand around the man's mouth and the other round his neck. He put a foot on the bars and heaved, as if he were pulling a rope. The man kicked and thrashed for a long time before he sagged and slid to the floor. She took the keys from his belt and unlocked the door. She had never seen a man being killed before and the fizzing in her heart made it seem like nothing, like falling asleep, like the games her brothers played when they were young.

He took the man's sword and met the second guard running in. He swung it into his belly and lifted him on the point to force it deeper, then let him drop. He put his boot on the man's chest and pulled the blade out with a sucking gurgle. By this time his friends were pouring out of the barn, the men arming themselves with makeshift weapons from the walls, staves, pitchforks, iron bars.

He told them to make their way to the harbour, where he would meet them shortly. He told them to take her with them and treat her well. For a moment she thought he was going to murder her parents. He laid a hand on her cheek and told her that they would be safe.

He chose two men to accompany him and they ran towards the palace.

They said her mother had been raped by a bull and had given birth to a monster who lay chained and snarling in a nest of straw and dung at the centre of a maze beneath the palace, waiting for the young men and women from Athens to be offered to him as fresh meat.

Let the peasants keep their stories, her father said. They had precious little else. And it was safer to be feared than to be pitied.

But the story hurt, for her brother was indeed a monster in her family's eyes. His bloated head, his rages, the way he lashed out at the men who went into the cellar to sluice him with buckets of water every week, to carry off the foul straw and fill his trough with the same food they gave to the pigs, kitchen scraps, greasy bones, wine gone sour.

They thought he could not speak. They never asked him a question so he never gave them a reply. But she knew. She went down to the cellar most days and sat with him in the light of that single, guttering torch and held his hand. He would lay his head on her lap and tell her about the things that the men did to him for their amusement. She would give him fruit and bread that she had hidden under her skirt and while he ate she told him about the world outside, about the ocean that was like the water in the bucket but deeper and broader than he could possibly imagine, about boats that were like floating houses, about music that was sound shaped to make you happy, about the pines outside her window and the woodcutters in the summer.

He wept sometimes, but he never asked for help. When he was younger and she was more naïve, she suggested that he try to escape, but he did not understand what she was saying, for he had never seen anything beyond these damp walls, and thought her stories of oceans and boats and music were simply games to make the darkness bearable.

He was right, of course. He could not live outside. The sun would blind him. He would be mocked and taunted and stoned.

Her mother, her father, her brothers, they put him out of their minds. But she could not. She felt his presence constantly, like the distant rumble of thunder, like the shapes that moved in the water in the harbour. And when she felt the weight of his deformed head in her lap and ran her hand through his patchy hair, the kindness ran both ways, for he was easing her discomfort as much as she was easing his.

They reached the harbour to find that the captain had already hoisted six small barrels of pitch up out of the hold. There were flints and torn cloth and the men set the barrels alight and slung them onto the decks of the other ships and the sailors on watch were too occupied trying to extinguish the flames to concern themselves with anything but saving their own vessels.

She was petrified. She could see what it meant to be in the middle of a story, and why the men protected them from this. It was a mistake. She understood that now. A moment's weakness had caused this horror, the way a single spark from those struck flints bloomed into the fires that surrounded her. She wanted to turn back time, but there was screaming and the clash of metal striking metal and the splitting of planks and the air was black with smoke, and she had trouble even breathing.

Then she saw him running along the quay with his three companions, carrying a sack, pursued by palace guards and he was a hand reaching down to pull her from the hole into which she had fallen, and if only he made it to the boat in time she would be safe and happy.

They pushed off and the four men jumped the widening gap between the hull and the harbour wall. A guard leapt behind them and was struck in the face with a sword so that his head split and he dropped into the water, his blood spraying the man who killed him. A second leapt and clung briefly to the rail of the boat before his fingers were broken under heels and he fell screaming onto his companion. And then they were too far away for anything but angry yells which were soon drowned in the roar of the fires.

He turned to her and wrapped his arms around her shoulders and pulled her close and she could no longer hear or see the flames, she could only feel the warmth of his body and smell of his sweat. Then she looked down at the deck and saw the mouth of the sack fall open to reveal her brother's head.

She is woken by the biting cold and the sound of two hundred thousand birds taking flight. Waking to anything solid is a relief after the murky, cycling panic of her dreams. She walks to the door and sees the creatures that petrified her the night before, emerging from their burrows and climbing into the air like ashes above a fire, black backs turning into white bellies, the whole flock becoming a cloud of grey flakes drifting out over the ocean.

When they have gone the air is washed and white and she is able to hold the events of the previous day at a distance for a few minutes, as if they happened to someone else, or happened to herself many years ago. Then it all comes back, raw and real, and there is a spasm in her guts. She crouches and holds one of the guy ropes until the pain eases a little. She realises that she is waiting for something, holding her breath, hanging on. But nothing is going to happen, and no-one is going to come.

She squats behind a rock and relieves herself, and the sight of her own excrement sickens her, doubly so when she finds that the earth is too thin to bury it and the handfuls of grass she rips free just blow away in the wind and she is forced to use a stick to push it under the lip of the rock where she will not see it.

She drinks from a muddy pool of rainwater, retches and makes herself drink again. She wraps herself in the rug from the tent floor and walks round the perimeter of the island, a figure of eight with two stony beaches on either side of its narrow waist. It takes her two hours. There are no trees, only clumps of low thorn bushes bent flat by the wind. Green cushions of mossy thrift. Bracken and sea campions. Razorbills and butterflies. The greater part of the coast is sheer cliff, though in places the grass falls away to great slabs of cracked and toppled stone, stained with an orange crust above the water line and shaggy with weed beneath it. She catches a movement in the corner of her eye and thinks, for a moment, that she is not alone, but it is a group of seals lying beached on a thin promontory, half-fish, half-dog, their wet skins like mottled gemstones. The only signs of human presence are the remains of an ancient stone circle about which there hangs an atmosphere that scares her.

She returns to the tent, pitched in the low saddle between the two halves of the island and sheltered from the worst of the wind. She is hungry but has no idea what she can eat.

She wonders how long it takes to starve. She knows nothing about such things.

There was a ragged hole inside her, as if a part of her guts had been torn out. She kept asking, 'Why?' – over and over. Her brother was innocent. They had already escaped. His death changed nothing.

He held her till her sobs began to die down, then looked into her eyes. 'I need proof.'

'Of what?'

'Imagine there were no gods. Imagine there were no mysteries.' He looked round at the men and women on the deck. 'This is a hard world. They need to believe that there is something else. And they need this as much as they need food and water.' He wiped her cheek. 'I have to command these people. They need to look at me and see someone who has powers they do not possess. They need to know that I can kill monsters.'

He was not angry. He did not need to be angry. 'Your father killed twelve of us every year for ten years. Those people had sisters, they had mothers. Your father was planning to bury us in a ditch. I killed your brother. I could have done a great deal more.'

She had no choice. She had to embrace this man and put

her brother out of her mind. She had to throw away her old life and become a new person.

She wondered if this was what it meant to love someone completely.

The second morning, hunger wakes her before dawn. It is like a broken bone. Her body is not going to let her starve.

A cold drizzle is falling. She wants to stay in the tent but the pain in her stomach is worse than the idea of getting wet, so she makes her way down the scree again to the little beach. She stands at the top of the shingle slope and looks around. She has no idea if there is anything edible here. Her food has always been cooked and prepared. She has little idea of what this involves. She has eaten fruit – grapes, pears and quinces – but she has seen no fruit on the island. To her left is the seal pup's head, but that would need cooking and she has no fire and she cannot look at the object without thinking of her brother.

She tries to chew some seaweed but it is leathery and gritty and covered in a layer of slime. She finds some shells stuck to the sides of a rock pool but they prove impossible to remove. She wades into the shallows. The water is like shackles of ice around her ankles. She bends down, turns the pebbles over and pushes aside the fronds of shaggy weed, nervous of what she might find beneath. She wades a little deeper. Already her sense of danger is being eaten away by an animal need which obscures all other thoughts.

She is up to her thighs in the freezing waves now; the stones under her feet are harder to see and searching amongst them requires her to put her face into the water. Her fingers find a cluster of something sharper and more geometric than the surrounding rocks. She pulls and breaks it free and retrieves a handful of shells, speckled with stony mortar. She walks out of the water and discovers that the temperature of the ocean makes the air seem warm. She tries to prise open the shells but splits a nail, so she goes up the beach to a flat shelf. She puts the shells down, takes up a large pebble and cracks the shells open. There is a kind of meat inside. She picks away the shards of broken shell and scoops some out. She puts the contents in her mouth and gags. It is like salty phlegm. She waits and swallows. At least she does not need to chew. She eats a second. Then a third.

The air is no longer warm and she is beginning to shiver uncontrollably. She has five more shells. She carries them back up the scree towards the grassy saddle. She goes inside the tent, thinking that she must get warm and dry, but there is water dripping through the roof onto the bed and she has very little energy. She removes her clothing and wraps the deerskin blanket round her and lies down in the dry half of the tent.

She cries and rocks back and forth and manages to descend into a half-sleep that calms her a little. Then the stomach cramps begin and, without warning, she is sick onto the ground in front of her. She rolls over so that she does not have to look at it. The cramps ease a little.

He ordered one of the women to bring a cloak from below decks and sat her on a bench to one side of the boat, then returned to the other men, commanding them to fetch boxes and trim sails, watch for rocks and stow ropes, sending them to the rowing benches when these tasks were done to maintain as high a speed as possible. When they were out of sight of land, he altered course to throw off any following ships.

She had never been on a boat before. The cleanness and the coldness of the air and the spray coming over the prow took her by surprise. The way the deck yawed and pitched terrified her at first, though everyone else on board seemed oblivious. She tried to pretend it was a child's game, like swinging on a rope, or being thrown into the air and caught by her father.

It was the sheer size of the ocean which unsettled her most. She wondered how deep the water was beneath the hull and what lived in that great blue vault, and felt a nauseous tingle in the back of her legs, as if she were standing on a high tower and looking over the edge. She thought of how they were supported by a wooden platform no bigger than a courtyard floating across the roof of this other world, how none of them could swim and how they were all less than ten steps away from death, and she began to understand how brave sailors were. Or how stupid.

The thought of her brother was like a pounding headache. She moved as little as possible and watched and listened hard to what was going on around her, and tried to distract herself from the pain.

Finally the rowers broke off and a basket of provisions was brought up from below – olives, salted fish, fresh water and dry biscuits of a kind she had never seen before. It was poor food, and if she had been served it at home she would have been insulted, but it tasted better than any meal she had ever eaten.

He sat beside her but addressed her directly only once or twice. She liked the way in which she had so rapidly been accepted into the magic circle from which the others were excluded. He had to maintain a public face, and she was flattered that the private man belonged to her alone.

They anchored in the bay of the island shortly before nightfall. A small boat was lowered on ropes and three men rowed ashore to reconnoitre. They returned with the news that the island was uninhabited and began ferrying boxes and packets and bundles to the beach, taking passengers only when several tents had already been erected on the grassy ridge.

Nightfall frightened her. She had never been out of doors at this time of day. The firelight at home had always illuminated a stone wall, painted plaster, a woven hanging. She had never seen it eat up the world like this. The air was bitterly cold. She was losing her bearings a little and times and places began to overlap. She remembered the stories she had heard as a child, how Chaos gave birth to love and hell, how Kronos castrated his father with a sickle. And these things seemed no more or less real than her youngest brother, Glaucus, nearly drowning in a barrel of honey, or Catreus trying to ride a goat and breaking his arm.

They ate more of the salted fish and the dried figs which had been compacted into discs like little millwheels. Some of the men found a young seal on the beach and chased its mother away so that they could kill it. They roasted chunks of the flesh over the fire but several of the women found it inedible so she declined, deciding that she could easily wait another two days for proper meat. The sweet wine, in any case, had taken the edges off her hunger.

So novel and so consuming were all these events that she forgot entirely about the one waiting at the evening's end until he drained his final glass and took her hand and led her towards his tent. She knew almost nothing about what he would do to her. She had been told little by her mother and less by her brothers. She had gained more information by overhearing the maids' gossip, and they seemed to find it comical, though the things they described were both repellent and unnerving. She consoled herself that they were talking about men of a kind very different from the one she was marrying.

He closed the door flap and kissed her, for longer this time. She wondered if he would hurt her, but he simply slid a hand inside her dress and held one of her breasts. It felt odd and clumsy and wrong. She did not know what she was meant to do in return, if anything. Earlier in the day she trusted him to protect her. The stakes seemed higher now, the rules less certain. Her life depended on remaining inside the magic circle, and to remain inside the magic circle she had to please him.

She had already become a different person this morning. She would have to do it again. She pulled her mouth away from his and said, 'What would you like me to do?'

He laughed and lifted her dress and turned her round and bent her over the bed. The maids were right. What he did to her was indeed repellent and unnerving, and oddly comical too. She should have felt adult and sophisticated, but it reminded her mostly of being a child again, wrestling, doing handstands, turning cartwheels. It was demeaning at first, and dirty. Then it was good to be a child, to have no responsibilities, to forget everything that had happened today and concentrate only on the present moment.

When he was finished he rolled onto the bed and pulled the deerskin blanket over them. Within minutes he was asleep. She was unable to move without detaching herself from his embrace and she did not want to wake him, so she lay listening to the voices outside getting fewer and fainter as everyone made their way to bed and the fidgety orange light of the fire faded. Every so often the wind flicked back a tongue of canvas at the top of the door and she could see a tiny triangle of sky that contained three stars hanging in a darkness that went on forever.

Sometime after midday the rain stops, the pain in her stomach disappears and her mind is returned to her. She hangs her sodden clothes on the guy ropes outside the tent so that they will dry in the sun. She does the same thing with the bedclothes, and ties back the door of the tent in the hope that the wind might evaporate some of the water from its muddy floor. She cleans up the sick, scooping it into her hands and carrying it outside, then wiping her fingers clean on the grass. She does this without thinking and, in the middle of doing it, she sees herself from the outside and realises how far she has travelled in such a short time.

She finds the shallow pool of brackish rainwater gathered on the concave top of the mossy rock and drinks, and the coldness of the water makes up for the earthy, vegetable taste.

She begins to think, for the first time, that surviving here might be possible, but that to do so she must become like a fox, hunting constantly and never thinking about tomorrow.

Wrapped only in her blanket and wearing her sandals, she makes her way back to the area of the island where the thorn bushes were thickest and finds that her memory is correct and some of the plants are indeed covered in small red berries. She does not want to repeat the mistake of this morning, so she picks just one and puts it into her mouth. But when she crushes it between her teeth the taste is shockingly sour and she has to spit it out.

She makes her way down the scree to the beach, determined to master her feelings about the seal pup's head. But it has begun to rot and the smell is overpowering, and when she gets close she can see something moving in the flesh.

She has to make a fire. If she can make a fire then she can, perhaps, cook the shellfish and make them edible. She used to watch her brothers doing it many years ago, with tinder-boxes stolen from the kitchen, before they were caught and beaten. The boxes contained two stones and a wad of lint. She has no lint. But she has an endless supply of stones. She begins searching the drier, top half of the beach, picking up pairs of stones one after the other, turning her back to the wind, striking one against the other and watching for that tiny lightning. She does this for a long time with no success.

She climbs back up to the ridge. She is exhausted. Her clothes are dry but she does not have the energy to put them on. Instead she lies in the mouth of the tent, watching the shadows of clouds sliding across the surface of the water. There is a seductive comfort in doing this and she knows that the longer she spends without eating, the harder it will be to find food, but she can neither bring herself to stand up nor think of what she might achieve if she did.

He was right. Her father had done worse. She thinks of the bodies in the trench. She wonders if any of them were still alive when the earth was thrown back on top of them, and she imagines being trapped down there with mud in her mouth and the unmovable weight holding her down.

Perhaps her father was privy to events and information of which she knew nothing. Perhaps, seen from his perspective, these cruelties were simply the price that had to be paid to keep his people safe. She would never know now.

She has not talked for three days. She has not heard another human voice. Her thinking is becoming simultaneously clearer and more confused. Those concentric rings of the royal apartments, the public rooms, the gardens, the town beyond the palace walls, seem to her like a beehive or an ants' nest, some beautifully structured object whose working must remain forever mysterious.

There is a picture of her father which comes back to her throughout the day. He is standing at one of the big windows looking down towards the harbour. She is sitting at his feet, playing with a set of jumping jacks. His face is lit by the sun coming off the sea. He is not looking at her, but he knows that she is there. She must be three, four, five years old. She feels utterly safe.

Later, she would see him strike her brothers and, on two occasions, her mother. She would see him bring his fist down on an earthenware plate and shatter it, so angry that he did not notice his hand was bleeding. She would see him send men to be hung, and she would watch them weep as they were dragged from the room.

She can see now that her father, too, had a magic circle around him, and that she loved him less on account of who he was than for allowing her inside that circle when so many others were kept out.

The following morning she combs the beach again looking for stones that will strike a spark. This time she selects two of every type, then ferries them up to the tent where the air is drier and there is no sea-spray. She bangs them together in turn and her spirit leaps when she sees that a tiny star is born with a loud crack between two of the stones. She tears a corner from her dress and picks at it with her dirty nails until it is a tiny bird's nest of cream fibres.

Only then does she realise that she has no wood. She feels stupid, and scared by the realisation that she is losing the ability to plan ahead. She thinks of the effort involved in finding wood and begins to weep, but weeping is pointless, so after a few minutes she stops. She wraps the deerskin round her once more and walks around the island.

There are no logs because there are no trees, but she succeeds in gathering an armful of dry branches. She is walking beside the cliffs on the way back to the tent when she sees movement in the waves. She turns and watches two dolphins break the surface, curve through the air and enter the water again, then break the water a second time, as if they are riding the rim of some great, hidden wheel. They are heart-stoppingly beautiful, like long, silver bottles, or wingless, grey birds.

But they are mocking her. She cannot swim. She would die out there, whereas they can travel to ten kingdoms and back. For a moment she dreams of having their freedom, then realises how little it would profit her. She would not be wanted in Athens. She would not be wanted at home. Here is as good as anywhere.

The dolphins have gone. She returns to the tent, piles the twigs on the ashes of the last fire and rebuilds the little circle of stones the men built around it. She fetches the two stones and the little nest of cotton lint.

It does not work. The stones spark one time in twenty, and when they do she has no way of directing that spark into the lint. She tries a hundred, two hundred times. Her hands are bloody and bruised. Her arms are exhausted. The lint refuses to catch.

She is too tired to remain awake, but too uncomfortable to sleep. She drifts halfway between the two states, clipping the edge of nightmares and coming away trailing name-less fears that snap her briefly awake. She thinks that she has fallen overboard, or is running up an endless slope of shingle, chased by a nameless, seal-faced creature that is and is not her brother.

When dawn comes, she lies listening to the shear-waters taking flight. When there is only the muffled sound of the waves left, she stands and walks down to the beach, climbing round the rocks at the side of the cove until she is looking down into deeper water. She sits on a rock with her legs dangling. A compass jellyfish swims below her, a ball of light wrapped in a white bag with a charred rim, trailing ragged tentacles. It pulses in the slow wind of the current. She watches, transfixed. She is no longer able to measure time.

The jellyfish is gone. She stares into the translucent green water as it flexes and wobbles, much as she once stared at flames dancing in a grate.

There is a rash on the back of her left hand where the skin has reddened and begun to peel away. She runs her fingers over it. There is pain but it does not belong to her.

Clambering back up the scree she hears women's voices and a high metal chime like tiny bells. She climbs faster, but by the time she reaches the curved grass saddle, the voices have stopped and there is no-one there.

Her bowels clench. She does not bother to find shelter. She squats and relaxes and what comes out is a foul, orange liquid, so that she has to clean herself repeatedly with clumps of torn grass.

She walks aimlessly towards the highest point on the island simply to postpone her return to the tent. She does not want to look at the vastness of the sea, so she keeps her eyes fixed on the ground. It is peppered with the burrows out of which the shearwaters emerge. She stops and stamps her feet and realises for the first time how hollow the earth sounds, and how it must be honeycombed with little tunnels. She gets down on her hands and knees and begins to tear at the mouth of the nearest hole. The earth is woven thick with pale roots and she has to search for a sharp stone to cut through the thickest of them.

She digs further, making a deep furrow. She feels something scratching and flapping at the ends of her fingers and excavates the last two handfuls of earth to find two fat, grey chicks huddled in their subterranean chamber. She had hoped to find eggs, but it is too late in the season. She picks up one of the birds, a puffball of dove-coloured fur. It bites her with its hooked black beak. She stands up and crushes the head of the chick with the heel of her sandal. She hacks at the chest of the tiny bird with the edge of the stone until it peels back. There is blood all over her hands and tiny

feathers stuck to the blood. She bites into the warm innards, chewing at the gristle and swallowing what she can
tear off. She is eating feathers along with the meat. She gags
but carries on eating. Three mouthfuls. The bird is finished.
She gazes down at its brother. It is looking back up at her
with its mouth open, waiting to be fed, the black jewels of
its eyes glittery in the sunlight.

She stands up and walks away, wiping her mouth on the
deerskin.

She cannot remember her mother's face. She can remember
the faces of her brothers and her father. She can remember
the faces of the men who sat around the council table. She
can remember the faces of the four male servants who were
trusted enough to work in the royal apartments. But she
cannot bring her mother's face to mind.

This is the woman who brought her into the world.
This is the woman who brought her brothers into the
world. This is the woman her father loved. Yet every time
she turns her mind's eye in her mother's direction she sees
only the men she is talking to, the children she is playing
with, the maids to whom she is giving orders. She begins
to realise how little her mother did, how rarely she offered
an opinion, how the family revolved around her without

ever making contact, how small an effect she had on the world.

She begins to realise how alike they are, she and her mother, these blank sheets on which men have written their stories, the white space between the words, making all their achievements possible and contributing nothing to the meaning.

She realises that she can no longer remember what her own face looks like. So she leaves the tent and makes her way to the shallow pool on the rock. She puts her back to the sun and makes a canopy of the deerskin cloak to shield the surface from the glare. She stares down into the water and sees her brother's sister staring up at her, hair matted like his face, skin filthy like his, cheeks sunken, eyes dark, the skull starting to come through.

There is a storm at night. The thunder is like buildings coming down, and after every explosion the tent is flooded with a blue light that sings on the back of her eyes for minutes afterwards. She wonders if the lightning will strike her and wills it to happen, for everything to be over in an instant, but it does not happen. The canvas bucks and cracks for hour after hour and eventually she is woken by the rough cloth smacking her face as the tent collapses around her.

She can feel the force of the wind filling the canvas like a sail and dragging her along the ground. She has lost all sense of direction and is terrified that she will be hauled over a cliff. She is no longer willing this to happen, not now, not like this. She does not want to lie on rocks with shattered bones, or drown like a dog in a sack. But she does not possess the strength to wrestle herself free. So she lies flat and prays for the wind to slacken and eventually a gust hoists her free of the ground and she is swung hard against a boulder and the tent comes to a halt and she can do nothing but block her ears to the roar and the whipping of the canvas and nurse the pain in her side.

Morning comes and sunlight seems to calm the wind. She frees herself and rolls what remains of the tent into a heap behind the rock that anchored her through half the night. She looks back towards the square of dead grass where it had been pitched. The pegs have gone. Putting the tent back up is impossible now. She drinks some water, then begins the painfully slow process of dragging the torn canvas sheets down to the head of the beach, where there is some protection from the wind and she can wrap herself up at night.

There is now a constant throbbing in her head and a churning anger in her guts that she has no way of expending.

She lies down and closes her eyes and tries to get some of the rest she should have got last night. As she slips out of consciousness she hears the women's voices again, and that distant tinkling sound, but when she opens her eyes she can hear only the surf. She descends into vivid, fitful dreams. She is in the bridal suite once more, standing by the bed and examining the tapestry of the weeping woman and the receding ship. This time, however, she sees a part of the picture she had not noticed before. In the lower left-hand corner of the great, woven square, on the green of the island, she can see a band of figures. They are walking towards the weeping woman. She does not know whether they are coming to help the woman or whether they are hunting her down. She steps forward to examine them more closely and the dream evaporates.

The sun is overhead and the air is warm again. She decides that she must make use of what little energy she has left to find some food. Picking up the sharpened stone, she climbs to the grassy plateau where the shrubs grow. A part of her is in her body. Part hovers in the air above. She moves fluidly and, for once, walking is easy. She can smell the perfume of the small blue flowers and sees two gulls hanging on the breeze.

She finds the largest plant, breaks off the thickest branch she can find, then uses the sharpened stone to whittle a point at one end.

She walks to the place where she first saw the seals. She has no idea how many days ago that was. She simply assumes that they will still be there, and indeed they are, three adults and a pup. She sits on the grassy ledge and looks down. There is a drop, perhaps twice the height of a man, to the slab of rock that slopes smoothly down to the little channel beside which the seals are lying. Holding the makeshift weapon in her teeth, she turns round, lowers herself as far as she can, then lets go.

She feels, briefly, as if she is flying. Then she lands badly. The pain is so bright and sharp that she cannot breathe, only cradle herself and moan till it dies away, then roll onto her back. She examines her left hand. The little finger is bent backwards and will not respond to any commands. She cannot bear to touch it. She is sweating profusely.

She looks up to the grassy ledge. She can see no way of getting back. She looks down. The seals are still there. They seemed unbothered by her presence. She tells herself that this is good. They are tame. She can do what she came to do.

Her stick has slid down the rocks. She stands up, intending to walk over and retrieve it, but as she does so a flock of tiny, white insects swarms across her field of vision. She sits down and waits, then shuffles sideways, using her one good hand until she has the stick in her possession again.

She begins moving towards the seals. Two of the adults are watching her. She is fifteen paces away now. They are bigger than she had thought, their bodies thicker than the bodies of oxen. One of the adults nudges the pup into the water, then slips through the surface after it. She is ten paces away now, and she can see, for all their ungainliness, how strong these animals are and how much they weigh. She realises that what she is about to do is dangerous. She cannot remember precisely why she is doing it. But changing her mind and doing something different seems like the hardest thing of all. She is five paces away. One of the seals lumbers towards her, rears up and opens its mouth and barks. It sounds like the bottom of a great jar being scraped. It is talking to her, and no-one has talked to her in a long time. She almost says something back. These animals are going to save her. She wonders why she did not come here sooner. It would have made everything so much easier.

Putting her right hand flat on the ground she gets slowly to her feet. She is a little giddy but there are no stars this time. The seal rears and barks again. She grips the stick tightly, steps forward and shoves the point into the flesh of the seal's head. It moves with surprising speed, flicking the stick away and swinging immediately back to sink its teeth into her ankle, then swinging its head a third time so that her leg is yanked out from underneath her. The seal lets go and she is tumbling towards the channel. She puts out her hands but the stone is slimy with weed and she cannot get sufficient grip. She crashes into the water, her arms flailing. She's hunting desperately for handholds but there are none to be found. Her head goes under, she breathes a mouthful of salty water and coughs it out. She grabs two shanks of weed and pulls her head above the surface. She looks round, thinking the seal is going to attack again, but they are all gone. She wonders if they are circling beneath her, biding their time. She looks down but she cannot even see her own feet. What she can see is the pink froth and clouds of blood in the water.

The tiny white insects reappear, crowding in from the right. She holds the weed tight and breathes as slowly and as calmly as she can. Then her left hand slips, and as she lunges to regain her grip she catches her broken finger and screams and her hand locks and becomes a lump of hurting flesh and she is underwater again, her arms cycling and thrashing, trying to haul her body back into the light and air. Her sandals have slipped off and her feet are bare, and when they find a foothold she can feel the jagged shells slicing her soles. But her eyes are starting to fill with darkness and her feet no longer matter, so she kicks hard and hits that wall of air headfirst, arms wheeling and gulping. She grabs another braid of weed and the animal inside her takes over and she is moving sideways along the channel to the point where its bottom rises and she is standing in waist-deep water at last.

Everything hurts. She is cold to her bones and unable to stop herself shivering, but getting out of the water means lifting herself onto a seaweed-covered shelf. It is all of a hand's breadth above the surface of the water, but even that effort is beyond her imagination, and she does not want to take any more risks that might pitch her into deeper water.

The world slips out of focus, then comes back. She sees her stick a little further up the rock, the stripped wood of its point still red with the seal's blood. She remembers eating a baby bird. Was that yesterday? Or the day before? It is hard to be clear about these things. Why did she not dig another bird out of its nest instead of coming down here to kill an animal ten times her size? She has no answer to these questions.

With no warning, the water rises around her and she turns to see the seal breaking the surface only a yard away, and she has no idea how she does it, but suddenly she is out of the water and crawling up the rocky slope to prevent the creature attacking her.

She collapses and looks back, panting. The seal is no longer there. She examines her leg. There are two deep gashes on her ankle. A flap of skin hangs from the upper one, the size of her palm. Beneath it she can see something white. It might be bone. She looks away.

She went down to the cellar one time and found her brother's head covered in blood. She asked him what had happened, but he would say nothing at first. She fetched some water from the bucket and washed the wound, then tore a strip of cloth from her skirt and bandaged it. She put her arms around him and asked if one of the men had done this to him. He shook his head. She pulled back and looked into his eyes.

'Tell me.'

'I did it.'

'You did it?'

'I did it.'

'You hurt yourself? How?'

'Wall.' He nodded to one of the arches of the brick vault and she saw the bloodstains.

'Why?'

'Want it to stop.'

'What do you want to stop?'

'Everything to stop. Want everything to stop.'

She pretended not to understand. She can see now that she was a coward. She can see now that if she was braver, if she really loved her brother, she would have taken a knife down those dark stairs and slipped it between his ribs and let him die in her arms.

Night comes, and in the darkness, after the shearwaters have flown ashore, she hears animals that are neither seals nor birds nor jellyfish. She hears lions and leopards and wolves. She hears the clanking of chains. She hears drunken shouting and the crackle of a fire and something large breathing close to her ear. She hears the air going in and out of its nostrils and smells the rot of its yellow teeth. She feels the heat of its breath.

Grey light. Intense cold. A fine rain is falling. She cannot move her leg. She cannot move her hand. The world is a tiny, bright thing, so small she can hold it in her hand.

She looks up to the fringe of green grass high above her head. That was the place she had come from. There was a bed up there. But if there is a way back she is unable to see it from here. She can move her other leg a little. She thinks about trying to stand up so that she can find a route, but this rock is a kind of bed, too, and she has a memory of the other bed blowing away. She can smell the ammonia on her breath. She looks down at her damaged hand. The fingers are in the wrong place. It looks like a badly drawn picture of a hand.

She is in a garden. There are fountains and lavender bushes covered in bees that rise in angry, humming clouds when her brothers hit them with sticks. The nurse drags the boys away. She trod on a bee once. Her foot swelled and she had to put it in a bucket of hot water. There are bowers, too, where she can sit out of the heat of the sun. From her favourite one she can look down over the wall to the quays. She likes doing this. Sometimes she sees ships entering or leaving the harbour. She likes to imagine the countries from which they have come, the countries the old men talk about, countries made entirely of sand, countries where the people have skin as black and glossy as plums, countries where there are water lizards as long as a rowing boat.

She is playing with a hoop made of stripped willow branches, tapered and bound together at each pole with little spirals of thread. If no-one gets in the way she can run alongside it, batting it with a stick to keep it rolling, and do a circuit of the entire garden.

She is certain she has been in this place before. It is so familiar, but she cannot remember when. It is the most beautiful garden in the world. She never wants to leave.

It is dark again, there is a high wind and the sea explodes on the rocks below. The moon is full and she can see the waves coming in, each one a black hill with a crest of blue snow that swells and flexes and is dropped onto the rocky shelf, where it booms and turns to freezing spray that falls on her like rain.

She thinks how calm it must be under those waves, in that dark that goes down and down, where the dolphins swim and the jellyfish drift on the current and the forests of seaweed sway. So much better than up here where everything hurts.

Someone lives down there, under everything, and he is waiting for her, but she cannot remember his name or bring his face to mind.

Dawn comes and she knows that it is the last one she will see. The sun is out and that is some small comfort. Her throat and mouth are dry and she cannot generate enough saliva to swallow. Her lips are cracked and bleeding. She can see nothing but fog through her right eye.

There is a flock of gulls standing further down the rock, all looking out to sea, preening their grey wings with their orange beaks and shaking out their feathers. Their eyes are little yellow stones with black holes drilled through them. The ocean is beaten silver. The seals have come back.

She can hear the cymbals again, a distant, high ringing that comes and goes on the breeze, now louder, now quieter. She wonders if there is something wrong with her ears. Then she hears the faint but unmistakable sound of a big animal growling, that lazy rumble like a barrel on cobbles. The gulls scatter and the seals slip into the waves, leaving only circles of wash behind them.

Everything is briefly still and silent, as if the island is holding its breath. Then she sees him. He is a big man, naked except for a ragged cloak of red cloth, taller than she remembers from the boat, and more muscular. His head is too large and there is blood on his face. A lion and a wolf are padding at his side, the lion to the left, the wolf to the right. Behind him are six men and six women. They are naked, too. Some have made themselves crowns and belts of creepers and green branches. Some are carrying strips of meat, or freshly killed animals. Rabbits, foxes, pheasants.

He stands in front of her, breathing heavily. His chest and shoulders are covered with wiry black hair and she can see now that he has horns. There is dung on his legs and his penis is thick and erect. He bends down and picks her up. She can smell wine on his breath and the rot of his teeth. He licks her and she realises that he cannot speak. She recognises him from somewhere. She does not feel frightened. No-one can hurt her any more. There is no longer enough of her to be hurt.

He turns her over and lays her down and pushes himself into her. The movement back and forth inside her is the movement of the waves back and forth against the rock, the coming and going of the birds, the pulse of day and night, summer turning into autumn, to winter, to spring to summer again, the heart squeezing and releasing, the shuttle of the blood.

Then they are on top of her, the men and women, biting, tearing, ripping her skin, pulling out her hair, breaking her fingers, gouging her eyes, hacking out the fat and muscle, pulling free the greasy tubes and bags of her innards, till she is finally free of her body. Rising now, she looks down at the skeleton lying on the rocks, gulls picking at the remaining shreds of meat and gristle. She looks at the grass blowing in the wind, the fringe of restless surf, the island shrinking till it is no more than a lump in the fastness of the sea, the sea an azure tear on the surface of the great globe itself that shrinks rapidly in the haze of the sun as she floats into the great black vault of space, a cracked bowl of seven stars, Corona Borealis, the northern crown.

She is immortal.

Geoff DYER

Playing with...

GEOFF DYER (born Cheltenham, 1958) is the author of four novels: *Paris Trance, The Search, The Colour of Memory* and most recently *Jeff in Venice, Death in Varanasi* (2009). He has also produced a critical study of John Berger (*Ways of Telling*), five genre-defying titles (*But Beautiful, The Missing of the Somme, Out of Sheer Rage, Yoga For People Who Can't Be Bothered to Do It, The Ongoing Moment*) and a collection of essays and reviews (*Anglo-English Attitudes*). He lives in London.

IN MY FIRST YEAR as an undergraduate at Oxford – this was 1977–8 – I lived on the ground floor of the Corpus Christi New Building, just across the road from the venerable old college itself. During Michaelmas term, at about two in the morning, I was woken up by a gang of people singing Bob Dylan's 'Rainy Day Women' outside my window. They kept going up and down the narrow lane, singing 'Everybody must get stoned.' It went on for ages and eventually I got dressed and went out to confront them. As I did so I met my friend Paul, an American who lived along the corridor. We were both furious. Seeing each other like this meant our fury turned into bravado and made us more furiously brave.

'Let's get those guys,' he said. On the way out of the New Building we armed ourselves with empty milk bottles from the crate inside the gate. By the time we got outside into the lane the stoners were gone but we could still hear them, more faintly now. We followed the sound, crossed over to the college. From a first-floor window we could hear them singing the same chorus, the same song. If we had been back in our rooms we would not have heard them and could have slept soundly, but we were outside on the street, wide awake, furious and excited. Paul looked at me and said, 'Shall we?'

Without another word we threw our four milk bottles through the window. The crash of glass was unbelievable. We tore back into the New Building. As we separated, Paul shouted, 'Night, Geoff!' as though we had just done something exciting and mischievous.

As soon as I got back to my room the awful gravity of what we had done came crashing in on me. Four bottles exploding through a window: what physical harm would this have done to a room full of people?

In the morning, after an almost entirely sleepless night, I went out to look at the scene of the crime. The glass had all been cleared up. The windows were unbroken. Miraculously, all four bottles had shattered against either the walls or the metal framing the small panes. Not a single bottle had made it through the window. It was like a nightmare where you dream that you have done something terrible and then wake up, bathed in sweat, relieved to find that you have not done it in real life.

In the autumn of 1997 I went to Durham, North Carolina, to write about the photographer William Gedney, whose archive had ended up at Duke University. Durham itself is tiny, part of the Triangle Area that also comprises Raleigh and Chapel Hill. In the course of my two-month stay I regularly drove fifteen or twenty miles to go to a cinema in the suburbs of one of these affiliated towns. I say suburbs but, at night, it felt like driving in the open country, along deserted roads in complete darkness. I rarely drive in England so the problem of driving on the 'wrong' side of the road never came up. Then, on my way back from seeing *The Ice Storm*, I did exactly that: drove up a totally dark lane on the wrong side of the road. I had no idea I was doing this until a car screamed towards me and, at the last moment, swerved past. There wasn't even time for the driver to sound the horn. The car swerved around me and was gone and I was unscathed.

Two years later I travelled to the Bahamas with my then girl-friend to write a piece for an American magazine. We had to change in Miami, entering the US before boarding the connecting flight to Nassau and taking a boat to Harbour Island.

After a few days on Harbour Island we started sniffing around, trying to buy grass. The Bahamas is not like Jamaica where every few minutes someone is asking – to put it mildly – if you would like to buy sensei. There were quite a few dreadlocked young guys with whom we exchanged glances, but we never quite approached anyone. Bahamians are big drinkers but Harbour Island didn't seem like a stoner scene and my policy, in these matters, is to be cautious to the point of paranoia.

We had been on the island three days. As I was putting on a pair of trousers – cargo pants, to use the correct sartorial term – I had not worn since the flight I felt something bulky in my pocket: a large bag of skunk complete with pipe. Accidentally I had taken this through what is probably the most drug-alert airport in the world – Miami. There were sniffer dogs everywhere. I had walked though emigration in UK, sauntered through immigration in the US, strolled through US emigration, boarded a plane to Nassau and entered the Bahamas. And nothing had happened.

This occurred during a phase when I was smoking a lot of the skunk that was in the process of gaining complete market domination in the UK. The immediate cause for my unwitting bit of smuggling was that on the Saturday night before flying out I had worn these trousers to a Return to the Source party.

My girlfriend was understandably furious. How could I have been so stupid, forgetful? Because I was smoking lots of skunk. It was doing to me what it is apparently doing to teenagers up and down the country: rotting the brain. Her anger was understandable and not entirely convincing. My forgetfulness meant that we now had exactly what we wanted: grass. We could get stoned. In fact we *had* to get stoned because I did not want to repeat, in reverse order, the process of smuggling, especially now that I would be doing so consciously (i.e. conspicuously).

What would have been the consequences of each of these episodes turning out not as they did, but as, in all probability, they *should* have done?

In the case of the Oxford incident, apart from the injuries I might have caused, I would almost certainly have been caught due to Paul's calling out my name. (In the morning the woman who cleaned my room – a scout, in Oxford parlance – said that whoever had thrown the bottles had run back into New Building.) I would have been sent down. If there had been injuries, presumably some kind of criminal prosecution would have followed. So I would have been sent down and I would have been in more trouble with the police (I had actually gone up to Oxford on bail, for criminal damage, but that is another story). Now, students get sent down from Oxford the whole time and go on to lead interesting lives. But if I had been sent down I would not have travelled abroad or done anything adventurous; I would have gone back to my home town and re-applied for the boring job in the Mercantile & General Re-insurance Company that I was doing during the nine months between school and university.

In North Carolina the consequences would have been much more straightforward. I would have been killed, paralysed, brain-damaged or injured. I might have killed, paralysed, brain damaged or injured the other driver. I would have wrecked two cars. If I had survived I would, presumably, have faced some kind of massive lawsuit.

If I had been caught with that big bag of grass in Miami, then, most immediately, we would not have had our trip in the Bahamas. I would not have been able to complete my assignment for a prestigious American magazine and so would have forsaken my fee. All small beer compared with what would, surely, have been the eventual outcome: being jailed in the US.

None of these things happened. I didn't get sent down from Oxford, I didn't die in North Carolina and I didn't go to jail in Florida. I completed my degree, as a result of which my life options expanded to the extent that I ended up becoming a writer who was invited to Durham and sent on a luxurious, all-expenses-paid trip with my girlfriend to the Bahamas. Life turned out extremely nicely, thank you.

When he was considering promoting one of his soldiers, Napoleon famously asked, 'And does he have luck?' I have got into the habit of thinking of myself as an extremely unlucky person. I could compile a huge list of all the ways in which my luck has been bad. I mean, how many times has it started raining within minutes of my beginning a tennis match? But these three incidents are examples, obviously, of *good* luck. They are incidents which you would expect to have quite terrible, life-shattering or life-ending consequences. It's not just that I was given a second chance; I was given a third and a fourth as well. If I were a cat each of these incidents would have used up a life: three down, six to go.

As far as I can remember these are the three luckiest things that have ever happened to me – more exactly, the three luckiest things that have *not* happened to me. Thinking of any of them now fills me retrospective dread. I have never done anything where the immediate and expected consequences could have been anything like as bad. I had a certain amount of random, unprotected heterosexual sex in the 1980s and 1990s but the chances of getting AIDS was minimal compared with the chances of facing the consequences of these actions. Put it this way: given the limited extent of my sexual adventures I would have been extremely *un*lucky to have contracted HIV. These three incidents, on the other hand, would be the equivalent of having unprotected sex with a promiscuous gay, intravenous drug-user – the kind of thing, I guess, that might well befall someone who ends up in prison in Miami.

I would estimate that it was about ninety-nine per cent certain that I would pay the price for my actions. But I didn't. I got away with all three of them, scot-free, without a scratch. Did I learn anything from them? I don't think I did. Or at least I didn't learn anything that I didn't already know: not to throw bottles through people's windows, not to drive on the wrong side of the road, not to carry smelly, illegal drugs into the US; in sum, *not to be stupid*.

So I ask myself the Dirty Harry question: do I feel lucky? *'Well, do ya, punk?'* Not particularly, no.

And what about fate? Or destiny? Can one draw a larger conclusion? Only that most people reading this could put together their own list of three similar episodes. There are a few others who, even by cat standards, have been super-lucky, have not used up even one of their nine lives. And there are some who are not reading this precisely because they could not put a similar list together, because they did not have my kind of luck. Irrespective of whether these things had anything to do with my volition, they have turned out to be my three enduring achievements.

Aflame in Athens

VICTORIA HISLOP read English at Oxford before becoming a travel writer, doing features for the *Sunday Telegraph*, the *Mail on Sunday*, *House & Garden* and *Woman & Home*. Her first novel, *The Island* (2005), topped book charts in the UK and also in Greece, where it was set; it has since been published in twenty-five other languages. Her second novel, *The Return* (2008), set in Granada, has also been a number one bestseller. She lives in Kent, with her husband and their two children.

IRINI HURRIED THROUGH the quiet streets of Plaka and the sound of her heels resonated off the smooth marble paving slabs. The exposed metal tips clacking on the ancient paving slabs grated on her ear but she had no time to visit the cobbler now. Trainers had not been appropriate today and these were her only pair of smart shoes and the only footwear that went with her neat green coat.

In this old part of Athens, racks of fading postcards had been optimistically set down on the pavement, carried outside each morning by the owners of the shops, who seemed unbothered that the summer tourists had now gone home and that they were unlikely to sell more than a handful each day. They were still resolutely hanging out their Parthenon T-shirts, posters with quotes from Aristotle and maps of the islands, and knew their expensive copies of museum artefacts would be dusted but not sold.

Irini enjoyed walking through this city. To her it was still new and she loved to get lost in the narrow streets that would lead her to the centre of Athens and its long, wide avenues.

It was her godmother's saint's day and she was on her way to meet her at one of Athens' smartest cafés, Zonars. 'Don't forget to buy her some flowers,' her mother had nagged down the telephone the previous night. 'And don't be late for her.' Even from hundreds of kilometres away in Kilkis, Irini's parents dictated the minutiae of her life and Irini, always dutiful, had done as instructed and carried an ornately wrapped arrangement of carnations.

The streets were quiet that morning and it was only when she saw several groups of police loitering, chatting, smoking and murmuring into walkie-talkies, that she remembered why some of the main streets had been closed to traffic. There was to be a march that day.

The traffic had been diverted away from the centre in good time. It was uncannily peaceful. For once there was no impatient honking of car horns, no whining of scooters to break the silence and you could almost hear the paving stones breathe. The streets were rarely empty like this. Whether it was four in the afternoon or four in the morning, there would be queues of cars revving at the lights, impatient to get home. Only demonstrations could halt the Athens traffic.

By the time Irini reached her destination in Panepistimiou, one of the long avenues that led down to the main square of Syntagma, she could hear a low, distant rumble. She noticed the police stirring into action, stubbing out half-smoked cigarettes with the heel of a boot and picking up riot shields that had been leaning against shop windows. That almost imperceptible sound would soon turn into a roar.

Irini quickened her pace and soon the café was in sight. Pushing against the heavy glass door, she went inside. Oblivious to the ever-increasing noise in the street, well-heeled customers continued to drink their coffee, served by uniformed waiters.

Irini's *nona*, Dimitra, was already seated at one of the tables by the window, elegant in her red suit, heavy gold earrings and freshly coiffed hair. She was delighted to see her goddaughter. 'You look so well! So smart!' she cried. 'How is university? How are your parents? Are your grandparents well?' One question tumbled out after another.

It was only a few weeks since her term had begun and Irini was still forming her impressions, getting accustomed to this new life, away from her sleepy home town in the north and the tight control of a strict father who had regulated the details of her existence. She had not stepped entirely outside the cloister of family life, however.

'Why pay for some tatty flat', her father had boomed, 'when your grandparents only live half an hour from university?'

For this reason, like many undergraduates, Irini was in an apartment which had been familiar to her for all nineteen years of her life, with pastel-coloured stuffed toys neatly lined up on her pillow and childhood picture books in rows next to her philology textbooks. Every object, on every surface, including the small vases of silk flowers, was perched on a circle of lace crocheted by her grandmother.

It already stretched her parents' means to be putting her through university, so she had been obliged to admit this was a good solution. Her father had a government pension which meant that they were not hard up, but any savings had already been spent on giving his children all the private tuition they had needed after school. Like most Greeks, they were fiercely ambitious for their offspring.

It almost hurt to see her brother's graduation photograph in pride of place above her grandparents' electric fire, knowing that they would be so happy when they had another to place next to it. Her grandmother had already bought the matching frame.

'Why do you have so many pictures of us?' she asked one day as they sat at the mahogany dining table.

'For when you aren't here,' answered her grandmother.

'But I'm always here!' she replied.

'Not in the day,' interrupted her grandfather. 'You aren't here in the day.'

In that moment, she felt suffocated, strangled, by the all-encompassing security her family gave her.

'It's great. I'm really enjoying everything ... a little strange some of it, but it's good, it's good. I'm getting used to it all,' she replied to her *nona*. 'My grandmother's *dolmadakia* are the best in the world.'

Every child was brought up to think that their grandmother's stuffed vine leaves were second to none and Irini was no different. They ordered their coffee *metrio*, slightly sweet, and small pastries and chatted about lectures and the syllabus.

From their table by the window, Irini had a good view up the street and she noticed that a group of photographers had gathered outside Zonars. As the phalanx of marchers approached, their cameras flashed in the faces of those who led the march. They were hungry for the following day's front-page picture.

The noise from the street was muffled by the dense plate glass that separated the customers of the café from the outside world, but there was a growing sense of threat as the close-packed group of perhaps a thousand students moved steadily closer and now passed in front of them.

The procession had swept along with it a number of large shaggy dogs. These strays and mongrels that roamed the streets, slept in doorways and lived off restaurant scraps were spinning around, barking and yelping at the head of the crowd. A few had been adopted and were held in check by a metre of string, and the canine over-excitement lent chaos to the scene.

The waiters in Zonars stopped working to watch them pass. Their neat, retro outfits and the tidy rows of gleaming tables seemed a world away from the shambolic crowd that walked by on the other side of the plate glass.

Young men largely formed the brigade of marchers and were almost uniformly in leather jackets, with unshaven faces and closely cropped hair. Their low voices chanted but it was impossible to make out what they were saying and the lettering on their banners was equally incomprehensible. On some of them the fabric was ripped, by accident or design it was impossible to tell, but it added to the sense of potential violence.

'Something to do with education reforms,' muttered the waiter in answer to Dimitra's question, as he scattered her change into a metal saucer on her table.

Irini felt slightly uncomfortable sitting here in this bourgeois café. She too was a student, like the people outside, but the divide seemed immense.

Dimitra noticed her expression change and realised that her god-daughter's attention had drifted away.

'What is it?' she said with concern. 'You mustn't worry about these demonstrations. I know they don't happen in Kilkis but they're a day-to-day occurrence here. These tatty students are always taking to the streets, protesting about something or other.'

She gave a dismissive wave with her hand and Irini felt a gulf open up between herself and her elegant godmother. It seemed wrong to belittle whatever it was that the people outside clearly felt strongly about, but she did not want to argue.

It took fifteen minutes for the protesters to pass, by which time their second coffees were finished and it was time to leave.

'It was so lovely to see you – and thank you for my flowers!' said Dimitra. 'Let's meet up again soon. And don't worry about those students. Just keep your distance.'

As she leant forward to kiss her, Irini breathed in her godmother's expensive scent. It was like being enveloped in a cashmere blanket. The elegant sixty-year-old hastened across the road and turned to wave.

'*Yassou agapi mou!* Goodbye, my dear,' she called out.

She glanced to her right and saw the tail end of the march still making its way slowly towards the government building, the chanting little more than a low humming now. For a moment she was tempted to follow, but this was not the right time and instead she turned left up the empty street. Traffic diversions would continue for another ten minutes so she took the chance to walk down the middle of the road, placing her feet carefully along the white lines. Lights still turned from red to green, but for a few moments she was all alone in this wide avenue, completely and unexpectedly free.

Several times that week, her classes were half-empty as students took time off to go out into the streets. It seemed strange to her, in their first term of university, to waste all these lectures, but it was obvious to Irini, as soon as she stepped inside the foyer, that the politics on the street were as important to most of the students as anything they might learn inside the faculty building. Thousands of identical red and black propaganda flyers were posted on the wall, their endlessly repeated message almost lost in a hypnotic pattern.

'Why don't you come with us?' some of them asked her.

As far as Irini's father was concerned there was only one political party, only one view of the world, and to take sides against it, even in an argument around the dining table, took more courage than she would ever have. Communists were detested, anarchists despised. This was the view she had no courage to question, so when a huge group of her fellow students went off regularly and cheerfully with their makeshift banners, she could not join them. For them it was a way of life and they felt at home in the graffiti-daubed corridors where even the walls joined in the protest.

There were many days and nights, though, when marches and politics were forgotten and every student, whatever their views, ate, drank, danced and looked for love.

That Friday night, in a bar in the Exarchia district, Irini caught sight of a pair of green eyes. The low light accentuated their pallor. She smiled. It was impossible not to. A perfect face such as this made the world a better place.

He smiled back.

'Drink?' he gestured. The volume of noisy conversation in the bar was almost deafening. Irini and her friends joined his group and introductions were made. The boy's name was Fotis.

The evening passed, with bottles gradually forming a glass forest on the table and smoke curling closely around them. Irini was happy to be meeting some people from other faculties, and even happier to feel the strong beam of this beautiful boy's attention on her. On a raised area in the middle of the room, singers and musicians came and went, their prodigious talent hardly acknowledged by the throng of high-spirited young people.

At four, the bar was starting to close and Irini stood up to leave. She knew that one or other of her grandparents stayed awake until she returned and this pricked her conscience. Out on the pavement, though, Fotis took her hand and Irini immediately knew she would not be going home that night. She was always urging her grandmother to believe that she was old enough to take care of herself, and tonight she hoped that the sweet octogenarian would take those words to heart.

Close by, in a crumbling apartment block, built well before the invention of the lift, Fotis, his flatmate Antonis and Irini climbed nine flights of stairs. The walls were covered with a pattern as intricate as lace, but on close inspection Irini saw that the design was made up of a thousand tiny letters. Just as at the university, even the yellowing walls of the landing screamed a political message.

Irini resisted the urge to look over the low banister rail down into the sickening depths of the stairwell and was relieved when Fotis opened the door to their studio flat, where a trail of dirty crockery led from sofa to sink and the air reeked of stale ash. There was nowhere for the fumes to escape.

Like her, these boys were studying at the university. But there the similarity ended. Irini breathed in the scent of grubbiness, the aroma of this reality, this proper student way of life.

Fotis's windowless flat, with its low ceilings and dark paintwork, seemed far less claustrophobic than her bland, if airy, home, and this struck her on the first and on every subsequent occasion when they strolled back to his place after an evening in the bar. It was always with Antonis that they walked home, three abreast with Fotis in the middle, and when they got in, the routine was the same. Antonis would switch on the television and settle down in front of it, pulling his duvet out from underneath the sofa which would then become his bed, and Fotis would lead Irini into his bedroom.

In the narrow confines of his bed, she was scorched by the blaze of his passion. It was annihilating, wordless, and the muscularity of his slim body amazed her. This was more than she had ever expected from love.

Not once did she see Fotis during daylight hours. They always met up in the same bar, which attracted a huge crowd most evenings, and then returned to his dark apartment and unyielding bed. Unlike the bedroom in her grandmother's home, where a gap in the curtains let through a chink of light to wake her, there was no window here. It was the coolness of the sheets that disturbed her in the morning, not sunshine. The incendiary heat and sweat of the previous night had chilled the bedlinen to icy dampness and the clammy solitude made her shiver. Fotis had gone.

The first few times she got up and crept quietly out of the flat, careful not to wake Antonis, but one morning, as she opened the bedroom door, she saw him sitting at the small kitchen table. In these weeks of knowing each other, they had scarcely exchanged a word. Irini had sensed the possessiveness of an established friend and detected a whiff of hostility. It had made her unsure of Antonis and now for the first time they were alone together.

'*Yassou* ...' she said in friendly greeting. 'Hi ...'

He nodded in acknowledgment and drew deeply on his cigarette.

Though it was still early, he had put on the radio and the tinny sound of a bouzouki tinkled away in the background. There was a pyramid of cigarette butts in the ashtray in front of him and pale ash sprinkled across the table top like icing sugar.

'Have you seen Fotis?' she asked. 'Do you know where he has gone?'

Antonis shook his head.

'Afraid not,' he said. 'Not a clue.'

Slowly and deliberately he took another cigarette from the packet in front of him and, without offering her one, lit up. He inhaled deeply and looked up at her. She had not really looked at Antonis properly before. He had the same beard and almost-smooth head as Fotis, but in other ways they were very different. She took in that Antonis was broader, rounder, and with a nose that seemed disproportionately small for his wide face.

'Right ... okay,' she said. 'Bye.'

And, with that, she headed out into the pale dawn and walked the few kilometres back to her own home, shivering.

Her friends quizzed her about Fotis, but there was nothing she wanted to tell them. All she knew was that the temperature of her infatuation for him rose by the day and the attention he gave her when they were together was new and extraordinary. She accepted that a few days might pass without him contacting her, not even with a text message.

After one such gap in their meetings, she collided with him outside the university. He smiled his broad smile and took her arm.

'*Irini mou*, my Irini, where have you been?'

Disarmed by his friendliness, she felt herself melt beneath the warmth of his hand. As they walked to his flat later that night, he stopped to light a cigarette. In the dark side-street the bright flame of his lighter cast sinister dancing shadows across his face. It was ghoulish, macabre, but no more than a trick of light.

The following dawn, she woke as before to find him gone. Once again, she found Antonis keeping vigil at the kitchen table.

'Don't either of you two need any sleep?' she asked Antonis, trying to make light of it. 'Are you insomniacs or something?'

'Nope,' said Antonis. 'You're not even warm.'

'Right. Well, never mind. It's just odd, that's all. Just odd.'

With that, Irini was about to leave, but Antonis had something more to say.

'Look ... take care. Please take care.'

His tone of genuine concern seemed strange and she had no idea what to make of it.

Classes at university began to become increasingly disrupted. Even when students turned up to seminars, the professors were not always there to teach and, if they were, some of them seemed disappointed in those that had turned up.

'So you're not on the march?' one of them asked her. 'Why?'

Irini had no answer. Explaining why she was *not* doing something seemed much harder than justifying why she was.

'I had your seminar to attend,' was all she could think of to say.

The real reason was her fear of her father's reaction if she decided to go out on a demonstration. His disappointment would be bitter. And her mother would literally make herself ill with worry. Parading down Panepistimiou and being spotted by her godmother holding a banner was something she would never risk.

In the past few weeks, the reason for marching had changed. The police had shot dead a fifteen-year-old boy in the street and the mood was a new and uglier one. There were many more occasions when classes at the university were empty of students and the streets were full of protest. Now the demonstrations became more violent. In the city centre, the stink of tear gas permeated the streets, shops were being set alight and cashpoint machines had become blackened holes in the walls. Every capitalist institution was a target and even the city's huge Christmas tree became a flaming symbol of the protesters' anger.

One evening, after a journey disrupted by road closures and police barricades, Irini got home later than usual. She crossed the polished floor of the hallway and, through a scarcely open door, she caught a glimpse of her grandfather reading in his study. She heard him call her name.

'Is that you, Irini? Come in to see me, would you.'

Even though he had been retired for twenty years, her grandfather still had the manner of a government official and spent hours each day reading at his desk.

'Let me have a look at you,' he said, scrutinising her face with a mixture of love and curiosity. 'Where have you been?'

'Getting back from the university ...'

'You seem to be out a lot at the moment. More than usual.'

'It takes a while to get home when there are demonstrations ...'

'Yes. These demonstrations ... That's what I really want to talk to you about. We haven't ever really discussed politics, but ...'

'I'm not involved in them,' interjected Irini.

'I'm sure you're not,' he said. 'But I know what your faculty is like. It has a reputation, you know. For being radical. And your father ...

'Well, I'm not a radical,' she said. 'Really I'm not.'

Even from a distance she could feel the eye of her father on her. Irini knew that he would probably already have heard that she often did not return until dawn.

A newspaper, which had been the catalyst for this discussion, lay on her grandfather's desk. She could see the headlines: 'CITY CENTRE BLAZES'.

'Look at what's going on!' said her grandfather. He waved the newspaper in the air. 'These *koukouloforoi*! These hooded kids! They're a disgrace!' his voice had risen. 'They're *anarchists*!'

The kindly old man could quickly lose his gentle air once he was on this subject.

And then something caught her eye.

There were two images on the front page. One of the burning tree and a second of someone falling beneath the baton blows of two riot police. The anonymity of the latter was guaranteed – their faces were concealed behind the perspex globes of their helmets – but their victim's features were caught vividly on camera, contorted by a mixture of pain and rage. If his eyes had not been so distinctive, so clear, so pale, the image would not have grabbed her attention so forcibly.

She took the newspaper calmly from her grandfather. Her hands were shaking and her heart pounded as she looked more closely. It was Fotis. It was undoubtedly him. What shocked her was that in his hand he clung on to a flaming torch. This was making the job of the police, who clearly feared that they might go up in flames, much harder. The picture showed that Fotis's knuckles were white with determination. He was not going to let go of his weapon.

'You see!' said her grandfather. 'Look at that hooligan!'

Irini could scarcely speak.

'It's awful, yes ... awful,' she whispered.

With those words she put the newspaper back on her grandfather's desk.

'I'm just going out for a while,' she said. 'I'll see you later.'

'But your grandmother has made supper ...'

Before he had finished the sentence, the door had slammed.

Irini ran down the street, turned left and right and right again. This time her feet were soundless on the paving stones of Plaka. Twenty minutes later, she arrived, her chest tight with exertion, in a familiar down-at-heel Exarchia street. The outer door to the block was ajar. It had been kicked off its latch some while back and no-one had bothered to repair it. She ran up the stairs, two at a time, and reached the ninth floor, where she fell against the door to Fotis's flat, hammering on it with all her remaining strength.

A second later, Antonis threw it open.

'Where ...?' she gasped.

'He's not here,' he said, standing aside to let her pass.

In her panic and confusion, Irini only had two possible thoughts: that Fotis was locked up somewhere or in hospital. It took her some time to take in what Antonis was trying to tell her.

'He's gone. He's gone away.'

'What? Where?'

'Look, you need to sit down. And I will tell you.'

She allowed Antonis to lead her by the arm to the kitchen table, where she took one of the two rickety chairs.

'What are these?' she asked

'I found all of these in Fotis's room a couple of days ago ...'

'But why were they there?'

'He collected them. I have known him a while, but ...'

Spread out before her on the kitchen table was a series of newspaper cuttings.

'Pendelis ... Areopolis ... Artemida ... Kronos.'

As she read the place names out loud, she knew immediately what the link was between them.

'Fire ...' she said. 'All devastated by fire.'

'But not just that,' said Antonis. 'Arson was suspected with all of them.'

'And you think Fotis may have something to do with—'

'Well, what do you think?' said Antonis. 'And I suppose you saw this picture on the front of *Kathimerini*?' he added.

'Holding the torch? ... I did.'

'And look at this.'

Antonis led Irini by the arm towards Fotis's room. As soon as he opened the door, an acrid stench of burning almost choked her. In a small pile in the middle of the room a pile of clothes and papers had been burnt. The furniture was blackened, and the bedclothes still dripped from Antonis's frantic attempts to extinguish the flames.

'My God ... He could have set this whole block alight!' she gasped.

'If I hadn't come back when I did ...'

'How could he?' she said, her throat dry with the shock and the still-lingering fumes from the fire.

'I don't think he cared,' answered Antonis. 'That's the nature of an arsonist. He just wouldn't have cared ...'

Once again she looked at the picture on the front of the newspaper and examined the familiar features. For all those weeks she had only seen their perfection, but now she saw them twisted by an all-consuming rage and noticed again the devilish look she had seen in the street that night. And in that moment the flame went out. The memory of it chilled her, right to the heart.

A Family Evening

SEBASTIAN FAULKS (born Newbury, 1953) worked as a journalist
for fourteen years before becoming a full-time writer in 1991. Best
known for his French trilogy of novels (*The Girl at the Lion d'Or*,
Birdsong and *Charlotte Gray*), he is also the author of *A Fool's Alphabet*,
On Green Dolphin Street, *Human Traces* and, most recently, *Engleby*; and
a biographical study of three doomed young men of the twentieth
century, *The Fatal Englishman*. He also wrote *Devil May Care*, a new
James Bond novel commissioned by the Ian Fleming estate. This story,
'A Family Evening', is an extract from his forthcoming novel, *A Week
In December*. Sebastian Faulks lives in London with his wife and three
children.

ONLY A FEW HOURS EARLIER, Vanessa Veals had put five cubes of ice into a Victorian rummer, poured in vodka till it almost reached the brim and added some fresh mint, a slice of lime and a dribble of grenadine cordial. It was her second 'proper' drink of the evening, and after it she would stick to what she called 'just wine'. She took it into the sitting room, kicked off her shoes and sat on the sofa, where she fired up the television.

She lit a cigarette, an American classic with a toasted wheat aroma, and pushed her hand back through her hair, which had been professionally washed and dried that afternoon on Holland Park Avenue. Before abandoning herself to the evening, she ran a check over everyone and everything for which she felt responsible.

Max, the West Highland White, had had his walk and a solid two hours' barking at the end of the garden under the neighbours' window. Bella, her fourteen-year-old daughter, was having a sleepover at Chloë or Zoë's house. She had a sleepover most nights, Vanessa had noticed, but it was probably good for her social skills. Bella's school reports were not particularly good, but then she was not a particularly clever child. She was a mystery to Vanessa. She didn't seem to be interested in fashion, for a start. Perhaps that was because she was plump, but Vanessa didn't think so. She didn't seem interested in discos or parties or boys or shoes or money or music or whatever they were meant to be interested in. God knows what they did at these 'sleepovers', apart from eat fattening food and wear fleecy pyjamas in their sleeping bags. Bella seemed to have come from a different decade; Vanessa had once found her reading about ponies, for heaven's sake.

Then Finbar. Well, he was up in his room and she no longer dared go up there. He could make her politest inquiry look like a gross breach of his privacy. Presumably he was masturbating or something, but he was sixteen and therefore legally an adult – or near as made no difference anyway – so there was nothing she could do about it. He looked very pale, it was true, and was as thin as Bella was plump, but what was his mother meant to do: make him go to the gym, eat more potatoes? It was best to leave him to find his own way forwards in life, up there, on his own. It really was a nice room in any event; the best room in the house, John always said.

And John? Well, guess what, John was working late. And when he came home, he'd work even later. Vanessa knew he had a big trade on. She could tell, because instead of coming to bed at one and lying awake most of the night worrying, he didn't come to bed until some oriental market had opened or closed – and sometimes not even then: she'd find him at seven, haggard and unshaven with the morning papers in the kitchen, still in last night's clothes.

Vanessa lit another cigarette and sighed. She'd married John because he was rich and because she felt he'd make few demands on her. He had happily given up trading on the floor of NYMEX and taken what she considered a more respectable job on the energy desk in the bank's main building in Wall Street; he told her he'd done it for her, though she already knew him too well to think he would do anything unless there was a financial advantage in it. However, it was a useful fiction for them both: she'd taken the rough trader and made him into a suave creature of charity evenings; he had transformed himself out of pure gallantry and a desire to please his wife.

What Vanessa hadn't foreseen was either the narrowness of her husband's life or the peripheral sliver of it that would be set aside for her. He treated her politely and remembered her birthday and their wedding anniversary with small jeweller's boxes and silent dinners *à deux* in places of terrible expense from which she could barely wait to get home. She had believed that she'd like being left to herself, being independent, but had discovered that it made her brutally lonely. Although she did read books and did have friends, her inner resources weren't great enough to withstand the relentless, remorseless pounding of solitude. It was like the sea: it never stopped.

John Veals had no interests outside the acquisition of money. He didn't play golf or tennis. He didn't support a football team. He threw all colour magazines in the bin. He went to the theatre or the opera once a year if there was a certain and measurable financial advantage in doing so. He never went to the cinema and he thought television was a waste of time. A personal shopper bought his clothes. His idea of dinner was sausages and frozen peas, though he was prepared to sit it out over foie gras and Japanese beef if there was a purpose to the tedium. He disliked alcohol, though kept the cellar well-stocked for Vanessa; he had an arrangement with a wine merchant in St James's to make an automatic fortnightly delivery to the house.

He hated holidays because they kept him from the markets and he had nothing to do beside the pool because he didn't read and had never learned to swim. He disliked travelling and claimed he'd done more than enough of it in the course of his job. The cultures, languages, art and buildings of other countries were of no concern to him. Vanessa had once forced him into a weekend in Venice where the only thing that piqued his interest was the thought that Jewish usurers had first begun to trade beside the Rialto; he declined to enter the Scuola San Rocco to see the Tintorettos because he had to take a call on his cellphone. In any case, he was allergic to anything that smacked of the religious. His family was Jewish, but he had no interest in their god or their traditions; in fact, he was himself consistently anti-Semitic in what he presumably imagined was an inoffensive way, talking freely of 'Hooray Hymies' – Jews who in his view tried to ingratiate themselves with upper-class Gentiles – or referring to his chief trader as 'O'Bagel' and even once dismissing a cautiously dull investor as 'bog standard Hendon Ikey'. 'My granddad came from Lithuania,' Vanessa once heard him say at dinner. 'So fucking what? Vanessa's grandfather came from Pittsburgh PA!'

It amused him colossally that Stephen Godley, a Surrey Protestant, had at one point found his progress barred at the Jewish-owned bank for which he worked. Veals claimed that before the partners' golf day at Pebble Beach Godley had been circumcised at the age of thirty-nine and walked naked up and down the changing room for half an hour after finishing his round. The only thing that made him laugh more was the thought of Bob Cowan, who had been promoted to the main board because people thought he *was* Jewish. He wasn't, but the Americans weren't allowed to ask – on the grounds that even to pose the question was in some way 'racist'. John Veals loved that joke; it somehow really spoke to him.

John had never, so far as Vanessa was aware, read a novel. He found all forms of music irritating and immediately instructed cab drivers to turn off their radios. He disliked art galleries, though thought the financial aspect of modern British art to be of minor interest; he admired the way that the collectors had first created the market for an artist such as Liam Hogg, then cornered it; such manipulation would not, he explained, be allowed by the FSA in any other commodity but 'art'. Although he understood horse racing and its odds as well as any man in Britain, he never went racing or placed a bet; he disliked the animals themselves because they gave him asthma. He had no social life outside the office, and Vanessa knew that he privately disliked his closest friend, Stephen Godley.

The only activity, the only aspect of human life, that interested John Veals was money. The odd thing was, Vanessa thought, as she lit another cigarette, that he'd made enough to last a thousand lifetimes – or, with his modest taste in sausages, with no hobbies, booze or entertainment, perhaps two thousand lifetimes – without ever getting out of bed again. Sometimes she pictured her husband's money: the millions, the tens of millions, the hundreds of millions, in neat bundles, in their original bank packaging, the faces of George Washington and Queen Elizabeth II staring into the void, sitting in a vault somewhere in the dark, doing … doing nothing, nothing, but just being there, promising to pay the bearer on demand … But what bearer? What demand? And in what life on this planet or one yet to be discovered?

Little Sophie Topping had informed Vanessa once in great excitement how Lance, her husband, had been told a banking secret – not 'inside information', Sophie was quick to stress, but a sensitive and deadly secret. Before he could be included, he'd had to swear to the man who told him that he wouldn't mention it to a soul. And Lance had sworn on the lives of his wife and his children. Sophie was flushed with shock and solemn excitement. 'That's what they do,' she said. 'When something's really, really, deadly secret and important. On the lives of their children.'

And Vanessa had laughed. A solemn vow for John would have been for him to make a promise about his children's lives with his wealth the thing on which he swore; that really might have been an oath worth witnessing.

'Why are you laughing, Vanessa?' said Sophie.

'I was thinking about John. I'm sorry. If you lost all your money, Sophie, and you came home in the evening and Lance said, 'Look, at least we're all safe, we're all well, we've got each other, we can start again' – well, you wouldn't be very happy, but it would be some consolation, wouldn't it?'

'I suppose so. But why were you laughing?'

'Because with John it wouldn't. Losing all his money would be worse to him than losing all his family. So swearing on them is no big deal to him.'

Vanessa stood up from the sofa and went down to the kitchen. Max was asleep in his basket, Bella was out, Fin was in his room and John was working. *Plus ça change*. She'd eaten salad at lunchtime so didn't need dinner; instead, she took two bottles of Meursault from the fridge, a corkscrew and a clean glass. Up in the sitting room, she closed the floor-length shutters, lit the wood fire, poured some wine and searched the television hard disk for the stored episode of *Shropshire Towers*. Then she lay back and tipped the glass to her lips, feeling the edge of loneliness recede.

The King Who
Never Spoke

JOHN LE CARRÉ was born in 1931. After attending the universities of Berne and Oxford, he spent five years in the British Foreign Service. *The Spy Who Came in from the Cold*, his third book, secured him a worldwide reputation. He is the author of twenty-one novels.

THERE WAS ONCE a Boy King who refused to speak.

He acquired his kingdom at an early age and everybody said he was just the fellow for the job. 'Look at his kingly brow,' his royal advisors whispered to each other, 'at his clear blue eyes so full of wisdom and authority, his kingly gait. Such a boy will grow into a fine warrior, and we will send all our enemies packing.'

At first they put his silence down to kingly modesty. 'He is being respectful,' his royal advisors whispered to each other. 'He is overawed by the presence of so many shrewd and bearded courtiers. He is listening and having his thoughts. As soon as he is sure of himself, the wisdom will come pouring out of him, just you wait.'

But the royal advisors waited in vain. If the Boy King was having his thoughts, he kept them to himself. He sat silent on his throne, legs crossed, and from time to time he tipped his crown with his royal fingertips while he listened to the counsel of his royal advisors. And just occasionally, for no particular reason anyone could work out, he smiled. But not a word escaped the royal lips.

Finally, his Lord Chief Chancellor addressed him in a tone of entreaty. 'Your Majesty, the hour has come to make war,' he declared, pulling at his silky grey beard. 'For ten years your royal army has done nothing. Your royal soldiers are fat and unmanly. Instead of fighting, they are making wine and singing and playing games in the fields with their children.'

Next, his Grand Vizier addressed him. His great gold chain of office glistened with emeralds and sapphires looted from vanquished enemies. 'Your Majesty, it is time for you to follow in the footsteps of your great warrior father. Enemy cows are trampling down your royal fences and eating the elderflowers in your royal pastures. The enemy's young men make shameless love to our womenfolk and are not punished. Enemy bees pilfer your royal pollen. Did not your great father shed his royal blood to save his kingdom's honour?'

And it is true that, at the mention of his late, brave father, the Boy King frowned, and stroked the ermine lining of his royal gown. But he uttered not a single word, although he had loved his father greatly.

Not one word to muster the fat soldiers in their vineyards.

Not one word to avenge the insult of enemy cows grazing in the royal pastures.

Not one word to punish the enemy's young men who made shameless love to his kingdom's womenfolk.

Not one word to smoke out the foreign bees that made so free with the royal clover.

The years went by, the King grew up and to the despair of his advisors married a common dairymaid whose only dowry was her beautiful smile. But how he won her was a mystery to everybody who had either forgotten or not discovered what love was, since he was never heard to address a single word to her.

So it was inevitable that, under the King's silent rule, the country should fall into a state of rack and ruin.

The royal fences were not repaired and after a while people even forgot where the frontiers were.

The enemy cows came and went as they pleased, and the King's cows took to doing much the same. Things got so bad that when calves were born it was not known for sure which bull was the father.

The enemy's young men continued their shameless pursuit of the kingdom's womenfolk, and the young men of the kingdom were obliged to pursue the enemy's womenfolk in return, and met very little resistance.

Thus many mixed marriages occurred, and many children were born who didn't know who they were supposed to hate, so they didn't bother to hate anyone.

The royal bees, weary of finding their clover occupied, decided to make do with the enemy's, and soon reckoned it as good as their own, or better. Some people found one honey superior to the other, or the other superior to the one, but no pitch battles resulted, nobody shed his blood for the honour of his honey, for the good reason that a King who never speaks cannot complain of his grievances or rally his soldiers to fight the enemy to the last man for the greater glory of the kingdom, even if not a stone of it is afterwards left standing.

Did the King speak to his many children as they grew up? To his beautiful wife with the delightful smile that seemed to shine more brightly every day? To the royal cats and dogs? To the royal parrot, who was so old he could mimic the voice of the King's great-great-grandfather?

I have heard it whispered that an inquisitive chambermaid once put her ear to the keyhole of the most private of the royal apartments, and overheard a man's voice making witty jokes. And since the King had only daughters, who could this male personage be, if not the King himself?

And once – it was the birthday of the eldest of the royal couple's beautiful princesses, and the whole kingdom was rejoicing and setting off fireworks and playing games by moonlight with the soldiers in the fields – the same pleasant voice was heard relating a bedtime story about a king who kept the peace by keeping his silence.

Into the World

XIAOLU GUO (born Zhejiang province, China, 1973) was nominated for the Orange Prize for *A Concise Chinese-English Dictionary For Lovers* (2007). Her recent novels are *20 Fragments of a Ravenous Youth* (2008) and *UFO In Her Eyes* (2009). She has also directed award-winning films including *How Is Your Fish Today?* and *She, A Chinese*.

YUJUN

Walking in a daze, I was captivated by a cloud speeding across the sky. My eyes blurred, my hair nearly burnt by the summer sun. I imagined myself becoming Nazha – the young god from the fables who has many arms and who flies in the sky riding on a wheel of fire under each foot. I was only seventeen. I could see myself as Nazha in a boiling hot big city.

I had just arrived in Beijing a week before and the sharp weather shocked my body. In the small mountain village of Sichuan Province where I came from, all seasons were wet and foggy, and I had to eat lots of chillies and garlic to keep me strong. But here, the capital made me restless and fiery, I ran aimlessly all over the city, looking at the huge Olympics posters on the walls and at the houses rising taller and taller every day. I was eager to see everything. I worried that I was too much of a peasant for a big place like Beijing.

Having no idea where I was, I found myself under a large sign saying 'Three Treasure Film Studios'. As the traffic lights changed, a flood of young men rushed across the road and into the studios. What are all these people doing here? I wondered. But then I noticed that they were hassling a bearded man, who was dressed in a long black coat like some powerful agent. He was choosing people. Just before he left with five young men, he saw me.

'Are you looking for work?' he enquired.

It took me a couple of seconds to realise the question was directed at me.

'What's your name?'

'Yujun,' I answered.

'Come with me,' the powerful man ordered.

'Where to?'

Someone answered, 'To move props for a film – we get fifty yuan and two meals a day.'

Luck has fallen on my head today, I thought, and I followed, obediently.

NING

My house cleaner, Yujun, got his first glimpse of the film world completely by accident. The job was easy for a young man like him – each time at each set change, he and other stagehands had to move props around. The movie was a period drama set in the Qing Dynasty and told of six concubines competing to be the Emperor's favourite. The biggest prop was a portable temple, which was used as the background for any outdoor scenes. There were also plastic pines, porcelain vases, chairs and tables for the Emperor. Oblivious to the plots, Yujun kept staring at his props, ready to get into action at any second.

Yujun worked at the film studios for a few days. He didn't squander the money he earned; he didn't even buy any cigarettes. When he wasn't working, he would either self-educate by reading the *Beijing Evening News*, or gather with other labourers and listen to the Art Director's speeches about the world – housing prices, touring Europe, the internet. Yujun was mystified by the world he found himself in; it was unlike anything he had known in Sichuan. He was fed twice a day and got paid on time, and he could always look at the pretty actresses in their exquisite Qing Dynasty costumes. Yujun's favourites were a bunch of servant girls who attended to the Emperor's concubines. Only during their scenes did he err from his duties, silently crouching in the shadows, content yet in awe as the girls moved like swallows and sang like orioles.

But then, as quickly as the job had arrived in Yujun's life, the swallows and orioles flew from their nest, and the crew dispersed. A group of people who spent every hour together, and who called each other brothers, scattered within hours, leaving no trace behind. This sudden collapse disturbed Yujun. Again he had nothing to do. He lived in a kitchen backroom where his hometown buddies worked as cooks. They didn't seem to have a job for him, either. Yujun started to feel that he was losing himself in this city.

YUJUN

A few days later I returned to the Three Treasure Film Studios, and waited at the gate like a homeless dog. One evening, after some days, I saw my Art Director coming out.

'Don't you remember me? I carried your temple around last month. If you have any work for me, I'm ready.'

The man pondered for a second, and then he said: 'Well, I've just bought a new apartment. It needs to be painted. Can you do that?'

The next morning I was at the Art Director's apartment. I was supplied with tins of paint, brushes and rollers. All rooms were to be painted pink, except for the kitchen. I thought the soft pink was a strange choice for a burly art director with a lot of hair, but I kept my opinion to myself and concentrated on the job. I fixed a large crack in the bathroom wall, and I managed to repair his toilet. The Art Director praised me, saying, 'You're a reliable labourer, Yujun, I'll let my colleagues know about you.'

And indeed, shortly after that, I started to work in a fancy suburb house. There my master was a Scriptwriter.

NING

It was strange for me to have someone around. I have been living alone for decades. No cat, no dog; no living being seemed to be able to survive under my roof. The only living thing in my house was a potted palm tree that a director once sent to me as a New Year's gift and, as tragic as this filmmaker's work, his plant died in no time. I didn't want to have any cleaners in my house either, but some weird art director insisted I should hire a cheap labourer he knew. 'You will be so glad to have him; it's like having three or four arms,' he said. I thought I only needed one arm to write. He also said that his young peasant was very useful. Useful: that is supposed to be the most important quality for a man in this world.

YUJUN

It took me half a day to find Scriptwriter Ning's house. He lived in a brand new suburb estate – Gathering Dragon Garden. There were some guards working by the gate, and others wandering around in their uniform. They spoke dialect, like me, and seemed to be doing nothing apart from making sure no beggars passed the gate.

Perhaps it was because I had never met a scriptwriter before, or because everybody else I knew in the movies only shouted and swore loudly, but anyhow, I was very impressed by the Scriptwriter. I immediately felt that he would teach me a lot about life. Ning was in his fifties, his pair of thick glasses giving him a scholarly air. Thin and bony, his hair was closely sheared like a monk's. Most of the time he sat at home, wrapped in a luxurious white robe. He seemed to live alone. That was bizarre for me, to see a man in his fifties living alone. Where were his wife or children? And his parents?

That first day, Scriptwriter Ning gave me a brief tour of his house. The living room where he spent most of his time was large. As the sun shone in between the curtains, I could see thousands of specks of dust floating about. The four walls were completely covered by bookshelves and an antique typewriter was tucked away in a corner: I looked at it in admiration, trying not to inhale the thick dust on its surface. In the centre of the room was a table so gigantic it took up half the space.

That table was the most important presence in the house. On it stood a silver laptop with a roll of beige machines behind it: the printer, the scanner, the telephone and the fax machine. Tall piles of bound manuscripts were scattered on the table, bearing mysterious titles like *Death* by Radiation, *The Garden of a Dunce, My Life as a Light Bulb Salesman, A Modern Romance – Love of Money, Sensations in Criminal Investigation* and *Trust Me I'm a Policeman*. And each was numbered: 'Draft 3', 'Draft 4', 'Draft 5' and so on. I wanted to read them all, but I was there to work, I was there to clean the Scriptwriter's windows, mop his floor and empty his garbage bin. I knew my place; I was just a young peasant. I didn't have the time or the nerve to sprawl on the sofa and read. Besides, with my limited education, I wasn't sure I could understand those characters.

The Scriptwriter seemed to dislike speaking, but his face was so expressive that I got to know him just by watching him. I knew that when the skin between his eyebrows sagged, he was not to be disturbed. And when his cigarette didn't leave his fingers, he didn't want to have any food. I marvelled at his concentration; that a man could write so many words was already something my thick thumbs couldn't do. I called Ning 'the Script Master'.

NING

On that first day when Yujun entered my house, he seemed shy, and he didn't know where to put his feet and hands. He just stared at my grand table with a confused face. I don't think he understood what my job was. He started to sneeze; perhaps the old books and the dust didn't suit him? My house smells of musty paper and reeks of tobacco. I love that mixed smell.

At first, Yujun's tasks were menial. He cooked and swept and wiped and washed and scrubbed, but I was scared that he would touch my manuscripts, or that he might clear my old papers into a dustbin.

We spoke very little; there was nothing to be said, as far as I concerned. But then when he started to call me the Script Master, I became uneasy.

'Don't call me Script Master,' I would tell him. 'I am just pathetic.'

'Pathetic?'

Yujun seemed baffled. 'How could someone who has written all those stories be pathetic?!' he asked.

I had no answer for him.

YUJUN

In Ning's house, every object seemed to be hiding a secret from me.

The first time I opened the curtains, the Script Master's throat produced a peculiar noise that I understood was a sign of displeasure; ever since then, the curtains have remained drawn.

I studied the master, noticed how he winced at the slightest noise: the flush of toilet downstairs, the sizzle from a neighbour's wok, or the chatter of the bored guards outside the window. They all distracted his thoughts. I wished I could grow wings and float silently in the house.

After a few months, in idle moment, the Script Master began to talk to me. He said, 'When I was your age, I studied hard,' and, 'I wasn't like you, I had to leave home to earn my living in the city.' I guessed my master came from a wealthy family, and wondered if he could imagine what life is like when you grow yams on a mountain, like my family have been doing all their life. It also seemed to me that Ning's life was not real. He told me, 'I like to live in my mind.' I've always remembered that sentence.

But I respected the Script Master's lifestyle. Most nights I stayed until he went to bed, then I would tidy the living room. Every second meal, I would cook spicy Sichuan cuisine with lots of red chillies – my hometown style. And Ning seemed to enjoy it very much. I began to feel the Script Master's home was mine. Sometimes, I picked a book from the shelf and studied. Once I picked a book called *History of Sex* written by some foreigner, but I understood not a single thing. Another time, I picked one called *Emperors: the Unofficial Story*. What I read in there stunned me: I would never have thought that our old emperors would do these kinds of things with boys.

Did my head grow bigger since my arrival at the Script Master's house? It had to. I was born a peasant, and according to my family book, eighteen generations of my ancestors had been peasants. But now I felt like I could maybe change my fate by staying with this man and learning from his house.

One day, the Script Master lent me a green bicycle. He asked me to deliver some manuscripts. From that day on I cycled a lot, carrying large volumes, picking up newspapers and seeing every part of Beijing. I even rode the bicycle all the way to the bottom of the Great Wall.

It was the tenth of September when I knew that my master was in trouble. He talked for hours on the phone, seething with anger. I had never heard him speak so much or shout with such ferocity. From the kitchen, I could hear his chair thump down on the rug at the end of each sentence. It sounded like Ning was arguing about his script. I soon realised that the target of Ning's tirade was a producer. He was cursing the producer, an 'uncultured' man. He shouted to the phone: 'You're a piece of shit. We all know you used to drive about in your "Get Rich" taxi and know more about horseshit than you do about films; every script you touch turns to pig piss,' and so on. I have to say that I've never heard the Script Master using such language before.

The argument carried on forever. It was about money. Scriptwriter Ning had spent every waking hour of a whole year penning a script and the producer hadn't given him a cent.

My master had been swindled.

The telephone was thrown back on the table and, swearing, Ning began to pound furtively on the keyboard. I tiptoed down the corridor and glanced at him. His brow was furrowed and his face was ashen. Writing truly is harder than labouring as a blacksmith or toiling in a factory, I thought. As a blacksmith or a labourer, you can't be cheated too badly. In absolute silence, I began to sweep the carpet. While Ning immersed himself in the work, his ghostly pale face gradually became streaked with scarlet.

The thump from the keyboard began to slow down until eventually Ning stopped writing altogether. He lit a cigarette, took a sip of cold tea, and began to pace the length of the table. Suddenly he raised his fists in the air and shouted, 'No more!'

I looked at him, and then I whispered, 'If I can be of service in any other way ...'

'Nobody can help me with this!' Ning's voice was horsey.

After a while, Ning changed his mind and he looked up at me with a helpless expression. 'But will you listen to my grumbling?'

He sat in his rattan chair and I listened.

NING

Sitting on a chair, writing day and night, is like being in a coma. The body becomes imprisoned in thoughts, the outside world can't enter. I have been in this coma ever since I decided to 'live in my mind' – to write. And this script, it has taken me thirteen months, day and night, to write the first draft, and then I spent more months revising it according to the Producer's opinions. But when I delivered the final version, the Producer just said it was a rubbish script and he refused to pay. As far as I can see, the Producer doesn't have the money to pay me anyway; neither does he have any budget for the production. He is a liar. He just needs my script to go around and hunt some money from rich people. That's what all these thieves from the art world do in China.

Yujun looked overwhelmed, even furious. 'How much does he owe you, Script Master?'

'One hundred and fifty thousand yuan. And if I don't get that money, there's no point in you coming back to work next week because I won't be able to pay you.'

YUJUN

I watched the Script Master sitting in his chair all night. The ashtray was overflowing, but I dared not disturb him. I cooked some dumpling soup, but he didn't have any interest in eating it.

The next morning the Producer called again and this time Ning went mad. After three sentences he smashed the phone. And after that the house became silent again.

As I swept the rest of the broken telephone from the floor, the Script Master grappled with the child-lock of a sleeping pill bottle. I was worried, so I took it and placed only one tablet in his palm. I knew most of the time Ning couldn't sleep, so why would he want to sleep today? I observed the poor man who had brought me into civilisation and luxury. Suddenly, I had an idea.

'Do you want me to rough him up a bit?' I asked.

The Script Master didn't respond. For a long while, he sat there staring at the swirling screensaver on his laptop, and then he turned to me. 'Rough him up how?'

And so we talked, and after hours a plan was decided: Ning knew the Producer was in business with a karaoke bar owner who made his money smuggling stolen cars into China from Europe. So, I would go to the Producer's and hide round the back, where he'd park at night. I'd wait for him to come home then attack him with a hammer. I would tell him that if Scriptwriter Ning didn't get his money within two days the police would receive a tip-off about his criminal dealings. My reward was to be ten per-cent of Ning's money; that was what the Script Master proposed.

The master found a hammer in one of his kitchen drawers. Holding it, I left his house under the moonlight.

NING

After Yujun left, I started to pace the living room up and down. I felt exhausted. I went to bed with a nervous fever. My mind was full of regret. I fidgeted uncontrollably and fought off constant nausea. I had written dozens of cops and robbers stories, I knew almost every type of crime and murder, but I had never physically broken the law. I began doubting whether Yujun could go through with the plans, and felt even more miserable than during the day.

YUJUN

Two days later, in the early morning, carrying a bulky bag, I rode the Script Master's green bike into Gathering Dragon Garden. No-one noticed me; the guards were still sleepy in their shed. I opened the Script Master's door. He was there, smoking a cigarette with bloodshot eyes, sitting still like a statue. I took the hammer out from my bag, and while I was washing the blood off under the tap, the Script Master remained silent. He just stared at me as if I was some sort of alien invading his house. I told him everything had gone exactly as planned, and assured him that no-one had died. 'Only some injuries,' I said. It was an easy mission for me – I am a strong peasant and a hammer is always a good tool. I told the master that the Producer's face had split like a blossoming flower.

Then I took out the money from my bag, and laid it on the master's table. Both of us kept silent. After a moment, the Script Master put out his cigarette, counted thirty thousand yuan and gave them to me – twice as much as we had agreed. I had never earned so much money in my entire life. I sat on the sofa, and started to worry about what I should do with that sum.

The Script Master looked miserable. He didn't speak, he peeked at the outside world through the edge of his curtains, as if he had met the last day of his life. It was nearly lunchtime. I opened the fridge and started to prepare Mala tofu.

'I don't need anyone to serve me, now,' the Script Master said.

I didn't understand what he meant.

Avoiding my eyes, the Script Master stared at the tofu and went on, 'I will call you if I need you again.'

I didn't know what to think or what to answer. Silently, I cooked the tofu, my last tofu for the Script Master.

NING

I was alone again, after all these months of having a young man around. The kitchen was less warm and the fridge stank and there was no-one cooking any meal. Dust started to accumulate on my books and floor again. I had a boundless feeling of emptiness. I couldn't bear to stay in this gloomy house any longer. And so, without telling a soul, I packed a suitcase and bought a one-way ticket to Putuo Mountain.

A month passed and my time in Putuo was peaceful. I didn't do anything similar to my past life: I read the Buddhism sutras, watched the birds flying between the trees, and heard the sea waves rising up and down under the clouds.

YUJUN

With the money I got, I went to a cheap area of Beijing and rented a small room. I found myself a table, and a chair. Every day, I bought a copy of the *Beijing Evening News*, and read every single word of it. I began to scribble; I wrote down things that had been lingering in my mind for a long time, from the days when I first arrived in Beijing when I worked as a cleaner in a luxurious suburb house.

One day I bought a green bicycle. I rode it around, and then I found myself passing Three Treasure Film Studios. I saw many young men from the provinces hanging around by the gate, hunting for some job opportunities. I thought of a story which began thirty years ago, about a scriptwriter, whose life started as a poor migrant from the province. I rode the bicycle back home, and I wrote down a title on a blank piece of paper: *Into the World*

Sandcastles:
A Negotiation

WILLIAM SUTCLIFFE (born London, 1971) is the author of five novels – *New Boy, Are You Experienced?, The Love Hexagon, Bad Influence* and *Whatever Makes You Happy* – which have been translated into twenty languages. 'Sandcastles: A Negotiation' is a work in progress from his next novel.

PHIL HAD LAPSED AGAIN. He felt too full, and there was still more food working its way through, yet to be registered by the time-delayed fullness meter. Three desserts had been a bad idea, even if they were small. The trouble was, the desserts were always the most tempting thing on the buffet, which created logistical difficulties when several of the main course options were too good to turn down. When you factored in that it was all free – or, at least, paid for – regardless of how much you ate, it was impossible not to go for the dessert, extremely difficult not to have two, and strangely easy to have three. He'd never done four, though. There were limits.

Joanna had been busy with Sophie as he'd gone up for number three, and Phil had been hoping she wouldn't notice, but when he was walking back with his bowl, and it was already too late, she gave him a look – an 'Another one?' look, with a raised eyebrow – that he found slightly shaming. He'd pretended not to understand, and had smiled back blankly, which he sensed just made him look stupid as well as greedy.

As they walked back to the room, with Ben between them, holding one hand of each parent, skipping, and with Sophie clamped on Joanna's hip, burbling happily away to herself, Phil momentarily thought, 'What could possibly be better than this?' For an instant, he saw himself as if from the outside, and he realised that this snapshot, of a man with his wife and children, walking happily through the grounds of a luxury tropical resort, looked pretty much like the guy who has everything anyone could reasonably want from life.

The holiday, after all, was perhaps doing its job. At last, they were relaxing. All four of them. The background buzz of annoyance and frustration and impatience that was like a perpetual tinnitus in their lives – so unceasing that he was barely any longer aware of it – had stopped. It was like when the fridge clicks off in a quiet kitchen, and having not heard the sound, you suddenly hear its absence when it ceases. Yes, the buzz had stopped. All four of them appeared to be happy and calm, all at once. This seemed, to Phil, quite miraculous.

The only grain of discomfort – other than the staggering cost of achieving this fleeting moment of contentment, and the usual ongoing sense of flatness and sexual desolation between him and Joanna – was his residual dessert shame.

'Why don't you go for a steam?' he said. 'We haven't used it yet.'

'Kids aren't allowed,' said Joanna.

'No, I'll take the kids. You go and have some down time.'

Horrible phrase, that. Down time. He didn't know where it had come from, and he hoped it didn't sound insincere. He also hoped that when she got back, she'd offer him a turn.

'OK,' she said.

That was it. Just 'OK'. She didn't seem particularly pleased or even remotely grateful, a reaction which Phil found both puzzling and galling.

Back in the room, having changed into her swimming costume, Joanna engaged in a long explanation to Ben of where she was going and why she couldn't take him – like he cared – and gave him a lingering hug. Sophie also got a tight, fond squeeze. Nothing more than a kiss on the forehead came Phil's way, but she did give his upper arm a little stroke and her lips mouthed a silent 'thank you' at him as she left the room.

Why she hadn't said it aloud baffled him. Did she really believe it would hurt Ben's feelings if he heard her saying thank you? Did she honestly think that an audible 'thank you' would give away that she took some pleasure in being away from the kids for a mere half-hour, and that Ben might follow this line of thought and be wounded by it?

She was crazy. Women were crazy. The way they felt about their children was simply beyond comprehension. Joanna had once told him that if she went anywhere without them, she missed them within about five minutes. It took Phil roughly a week to achieve the same sensation. He loved them as much as he was able – as much as paternity demanded and more – he'd found whole new reservoirs of love that he never previously even knew existed – and yet, when work took him away from home, and he knew he'd have a few days without screeches and tears and bottles and sterilisers and nappies and arse-wiping and tantrums and cartoons on TV and protracted meals of bland food, and constant disputes about the putting on and taking off of various assortments of diminutive footwear, and endless circular conversations about the minutiae of whatever mode of transport happened to be Ben's latest obsession, Phil felt a lightness rise up inside him that was the very opposite of missing his children. He loved being with them, and he also loved getting away from them. This, to him, seemed completely normal. That his wife didn't feel the same way struck him as masochistic.

He'd never confessed this to her, but he sensed that she knew, and he also sensed that she slightly hated him for it. When he was away, calling in for a pre-bedtime chat with the children, he always told Ben and Sophie and Joanna how much he was missing them all, and sometimes he really meant it, but he always got the feeling that Joanna suspected he was lying, even on the occasions when he wasn't. This had created an inflationary pressure on the necessary protestations of homesickness that were required to convince her he really was missing them, which made the problem worse, since the level needed to persuade her was now so high that it was perilously close to implausibility. If he said it and meant it, it now didn't sound like enough, but if he exaggerated it, it sounded like he was exaggerating.

This was just one of many thousands of little ways in which the length of time he and Joanna had been together had made it harder for them to communicate. If Phil examined any area of real intimacy between them, there'd be some similar decade-long linguistic slippage, thanks to which he couldn't say one thing without it sounding like another thing. Everything important had its own subtext – had so many subtexts – that whatever he said ended up meaning pretty much the sum total of what he had said on the subject in the preceding years. It was almost impossible to say anything new. Everything alluded to everything else.

At least he didn't have this problem with the children. For them, there was no past and no future. Right now was the only thing that counted. Perhaps that was why people liked children. While you were with them, they lent you their right-nowness – a gift that struck Phil as both trivial and profound, feather-light and heavy with significance.

'Right!' said Phil, clapping his hands together, more to wake himself up than to generate any enthusiasm from the children. 'Beach!'

The old guy from next door would probably be starting today's after-lunch nap. Right at this moment. Just lying down, putting his head on the pillow, and closing his eyes. How nice would that be? Just how good would that feel? Phil couldn't even begin to calculate the pleasure it would give him to be that man, horizontal, letting himself slowly drift off, with no-one to accuse him of laziness or neglect.

'You need your sun-suit,' he said, to Ben. Typical of Joanna, somehow, to have decided that although children had been running around in swimming costumes or stark naked for generations, suddenly that wasn't good enough. Ben wasn't allowed on the beach without a humiliating garment that had more in common with a wet-suit than a pair of swimming trunks. It was, needless to say, a huge hassle to get the thing on and off, and Ben couldn't wee out of it without a major performance, but that's what Joanna had bought, so that's what Phil had to root out and squeeze the child into.

The spare costume – just an ordinary one – was right there on the edge of Ben's bed. It was dry, too.

Tempting.

He could always plead ignorance. Pretend he'd forgotten about the sun-suit. But that might backfire. Pointless to curry favour with the steam room offer, then squander it all as soon as she got back with slapdash infant swimwear choice. He was being good today. He was trying. He'd hunt. He'd look everywhere in the entire room until he found the sun-suit. He'd do everything how Joanna would do it. Except that she wouldn't have to hunt. She'd know where it was already.

It was while he was searching that he noticed, with horror, the look on Sophie's face. There was only one word to describe it: bereft.

'Are you OK?' he said, tentatively.

She looked at him, her tiny features slowly contorting themselves into something resembling Edvard Munch's *The Scream*. No sound was coming out of her mouth, but it was clear that she was extremely angry with him for not being the person she wanted him to be, and was on the brink of going vocal with her outrage.

'We're going to the beach!' he said, enthusiastically, imploringly.

'MAMA!' said Sophie.

'She wants Mama,' interpreted Ben, helpfully.

'Yes, thanks, Ben,' said Phil.

'MAMMAAAAAAAAAAAAAAAAAAAAAAAAA!'

Phil picked her up, patted her, offered her a snack, carried her around, tossed her into the air a few times, to no avail. Then he remembered that once she was off, the only way to stop her was by doing something unexpected. So he put her in an empty suitcase and asked Ben to push her around the room, which he did very happily, and suddenly Sophie was laughing instead of crying, and everything was OK again, and Phil could look for the sun-suit, which he found just as Ben pushed the suitcase into the corner of a bedside table, noisily cracking Sophie's skull in the process, returning them, snakes-and-ladders-like to, where they had been a few minutes before. But at least Phil now had the sun-suit.

Phil comforted Sophie with a long cuddle, followed by a patiently spooned-in organic fruit puree, while Ben was appeased with the last two chocolate biscuits of the supply brought out from home, and eventually, half an hour or so from the start of the operation, they were all in the right clothes, smeared in all the right places with all the right creams, and all the necessary equipment had been gathered for the fifteen-metre walk to their favoured spot on the beach. Before they had even left the room, Phil was exhausted. And through the wall, in an identical room, that old guy was probably fast asleep. Then he remembered the couple on the other side, who were probably in bed, too: fucking. And there was Phil, in the middle, wiped out by the process of dressing and suncreaming two children, his last fuck and his last nap two memories so distant and hazy that he almost wondered if either had ever really happened.

Extraordinary, really, how quickly he could go from self-satisfaction to self-pity. Did this happen to everyone else, he wondered? Were other people's moods pushed around like this, like driftwood, flipped from here to there by crashing waves of inner bullshit?

As they emerged from the room into the blinding sunlight, Phil felt a glimmer of something akin to relief – alleviated envy, perhaps – as he saw that the man next door was, for once, not screwing his girlfriend, but was lying on a towel nearby, gazing out to sea. He had a book in front of him, but he didn't appear to be reading it. Then, on reflection, Phil realised that he was just as envious of this as of the sex. Well, nearly. What were the chances of Phil getting an unbroken hour – just one – on his own, in silence, sitting on a towel with a book, in the course of the entire holiday?

He picked a spot close to the shore and allowed his burden of beach paraphernalia to clatter to the ground at his feet, sending a stern reminder to his limbs as he did so to let go of everything *except* the baby. Ben quickly fished out the bucket and spade and began to run in gleeful circles at the edge of the water. What on earth could it feel like to be that happy? Phil had no idea. If he ever got laid again, perhaps he'd remember.

Clutching Sophie awkwardly to his side, he spread a towel onto the sand and put her down in the middle of it. She looked up at him with a who-are-you-and-why-are-you-here face. Phil made some baby-appeasing noises with his lips – pops and squeaks and raspberries – but she was distinctly unimpressed, eyeing his attempts at humour with a sceptical thousand-yard stare. This was the kind of interchange referred to by comedians as 'dying'. Phil gave up on his attempt at entertainment and sat next to her, looking out towards the sea.

Ben was already contentedly at work with his bucket and spade, so they watched for a while, until Sophie began to appear restless, then Phil decided to try another approach. He lay on his back and lifted her into the air above him. He instantly realised that this time, amazingly, he'd hit the comedy jackpot. She laughed and kicked, drooling slightly, which landed in Phil's mouth, but he didn't mind. There was truly no sound more beautiful than the sound of her laugh. He lowered her down, rubbed her nose with his, then pushed her upwards, causing her to laugh again, even louder – a baby laugh made not just with the voice, but expressed by every limb of the body. He did this again and again, until his arms ached, and she never tired of the joke.

When his arms could take it no longer, he sat her on his chest, with one leg on either side of his head. She enjoyed this, too, and bounced on him a few times, experimentally, before suddenly and totally losing interest in him and crawling off in pursuit of Ben, who had by now built a complex structure of interconnecting sandcastles.

Phil realised what was about to happen just before it did. He should have recognised that glint in Sophie's eye. It was one he knew well, expressive of the primordial human instinct to demolish vertical structures – an instinct that meets with endless indulgence from parents, and an explosive lack of sympathy from elder siblings. Ben, whose back was turned at the key moment, was irate at the destruction of his sandcastle, and pushed Sophie away. It was barely a push, really, but it was enough to topple her onto her side. She righted herself without too much difficulty, but then rubbed her face, not realising that she had sand on her hand. Within seconds, she was howling in outrage at the sand in her eye, and rubbing it harder, which ground in more sand, and launched her into one of her cycles of frantic outrage at the painful unpredictability of life.

Phil picked her up and attempted to wipe the sand from her face, but this just made her angrier. Ben, meanwhile, noisily protested that it wasn't his fault, and that he'd hardly touched her. Phil, his nerves beginning to fray, snapped at Ben that he had pushed her, which wasn't allowed, and made him the culprit responsible for Sophie's tears. The injustice of this caused Ben to toss his spade angrily onto the ground, where it landed heavily on Phil's little toe, sending an astonishingly sharp jolt of pain up his leg. Phil emitted a howl of pain and anger, which in turn set Sophie off on a new surge of her own howling, as if to remind him that *she* was the howler. *She'd* thought of it first, and she was not willing to be out-howled.

'WHY DID YOU DO THAT!' shouted Phil.

'I DIDN'T,' snapped Ben.

Phil found it hard to think of an answer to this.

'YOU … YOU CAN'T JUST DO THAT! THAT HURT! YOU'VE PUSHED SOPHIE AND YOU'VE THROWN SOMETHING AT ME, AND YOU HAVE TO SAY SORRY.'

'NO. I DIDN'T PUSH AND I DIDN'T THROW IT AT YOU. I JUST THREW IT, AND YOU WERE THERE WHERE IT WENT.'

'THAT DOESN'T MAKE ANY DIFFERENCE.'

'IT DOES. IT'S DIFFERENT. IT'S NOT MY FAULT.'

Intent. A knotty problem in law, right up to the highest court. Ben had an eye for these legal cracks and loopholes. He may have been only four, but Phil often found himself starting an argument absolutely confident that he was in the right, only for it to dawn on him, long after he could possibly back down, that he might be defending the indefensible.

'YOU HURT ME AND YOU HURT SOPHIE, SO YOU HAVE TO SAY SORRY.'

'SORRY!' barked Ben, with an intonation closer to 'Piss off' than to an apology.

Did this count? Could he really be bothered to press on in pursuit of a genuine apology, or should he bail out here, with this nominal victory, which was actually closer to a draw, but which allowed him (and Ben) to step back without conceding defeat or losing face?

'Good,' said Phil. He'd settle for the draw. He was on holiday.

'Will you fix the castles for me? The ones she broke,' said Ben, grabbing the draw and pushing on for a victory, sensing that Phil was on the retreat.

'If you're good,' said Phil, displaying a token resistance, aware even as the words came out of his mouth that they lacked all meaning.

'OK,' said Ben, nodding towards the spade at Phil's feet.

'Pick up the spade, then,' said Phil. He couldn't back down too easily. It was important that he showed he was still in charge.

'You pick it up,' said Ben.

'You pick it up,' said Phil.

'No, you pick it up,' said Ben.

Phil sensed that this wasn't entirely dignified. Nor, however, would it be dignified to give in.

'You're the one that threw it there. Onto my foot. If you

pick it up, I'll help you; if you don't, I won't. It's as simple as that.' There. Good. He'd shown him who was boss.

Ben instantly picked up the spade and handed it to him. Phil's sensation of being the boss had lasted less than a second. Now he had the spade in his hand, and he realised that he had somehow found himself agreeing to build Ben's sandcastles for him, which he had no desire to do. In fact, if it wasn't for their dispute, he would never have agreed to it. How was it that the upshot of Ben throwing a spade at him was that Phil ended up being nicer to him than if he had behaved properly? How had that happened? He couldn't remember, but he knew it wasn't right, just as he knew there was no way back.

He gently put Sophie down on the towel and began to dig. This manoeuvre did not go well. Sophie had now decided that she liked being held. She didn't want to be put down, and she was damn well going to assert her right, using the full power of both her lungs, to get whatever she wanted as soon as she wanted it.

'Sophie, I just have to do a sandcastle with Ben, then I'll pick you up,' he said, futilely. She could neither hear, over her own screams, nor understand.

'Not one. Three,' said Ben, with more than a hint of a gloat in his voice. He knew he was on top, and he was relishing it.

Phil didn't know where the number three had come from, but he made a rapid assessment of the situation and decided that it would be quicker to build two extra castles than to enter into a debate on the accounting structure of his sandcastle obligation. 'OK. Three,' he said.

Why did women like this so much, wondered Phil? Was it not a blow to the ego to feel so utterly servile? Nothing in his three and a half decades on earth had ever been quite so abasing as the time he spent with his children.

Sophie eyed him angrily and, with a glimmer of triumph in her glare, set about doing a large, wet shit. Phil could hear it coming out, and within a few seconds he could see it leaking from the side of her nappy onto her clothes and the towel.

'I'm just going to change Sophie's nappy,' said Phil.

'YOU SAID YOU'D DO MY CASTLES!' said Ben, instantly furious.

'I know,' said Phil, 'but first I have to do this.'

'You said you'd do it!'

'I know, and I will, but I have to deal with this first.'

'Why?'

'Because it's leaking.'

'Why?'

'It just is.'

'Why?'

'Because it is.'

'Why?'

'Because it's been a bit runny since we got here. OK?'

Phil had remembered to bring a spare nappy and some wipes with him to the beach, and he started to clean up his daughter, rolling the soiled half of her unpopped outfit up behind her while he did the nappy. With the nappy changed, he'd then think about how to get her clothes properly off with minimum smearage. The key thing was to avoid getting crap in her hair. He didn't have any spare clothes with him, a problem to which, at this moment, he could think of no solution. The idea of dragging them all back to the room was too arduous to contemplate. Wherever you went with children, there was always one thing you forgot, and that always turned out to be the thing you needed.

'Why?' said Ben.

'Why what?'

'Why aren't you helping me?'

'I've told you why. Because I'm doing this.'

'Why?'

'BECAUSE IT'S LEAKING!'

'Why?'

'Will you stop saying "Why?"'

'Why?'

'BECAUSE IT'S GETTING ON MY NERVES! AND IF YOU DON'T STOP RIGHT NOW I WON'T HELP YOU AT ALL.'

'WELL, *YOU'RE* GETTING ON MY NERVES.'

'Fine.'

'YOU'RE REEEEAAAALLY GETTING ON MY NERVES,' said Ben, trying out the new phrase.

'The longer you do this, the longer it's going to take, and the longer you're going to have to go without any help. Do you understand?' said Phil, turning and jabbing a finger through the air towards his son. As he did so, he noticed that the tip of his threatening finger was smeared with a dab of shit.

'You're just really getting on my nerves,' said Ben, non-chalantly, with the aloof manner of an aristocrat dealing with a troublesome serf.

Phil chose to rise above this and turned back to Sophie, just in time to see her squeezing out a second turd onto the new half-on nappy.

'OH GOD!' shouted Phil.

'She's done another poo,' said Ben, sounding more than a little pleased.

'Yes, I know.'

'You're going to have to get another nappy.'

'I know that, Ben. Can you just let me deal with this on my own? Why don't you make a start on those sandcastles without me?'

'Because you said you'd do them. It wasn't me that smashed them.'

'I thought we'd talked about that.'

'So did I.'

Phil didn't have another nappy on the beach. He really did have to go back to the room now. Could he leave Ben here? Would he be willing to be left? Would it be safe? Or did he have to haul all of them back, one whining, one shitty, in search of another nappy.

He looked up, calculating the distance back to the room, and the likelihood and possible reaction of Joanna turning up to find Ben on his own on the beach. Not worth risking. The fat woman from next door, the one with the perpetually dozing husband, was staring straight at him. As soon as they caught one another's eye, she rose from her deckchair and began to walk towards him. What the hell did *she* want? He looked away, but it was too late. She continued to approach.

'I'm Dawn, from next door,' she said. 'You remember me, don't you?'

'Er … yeah. Sorry, but I'm rather busy right now.'

'I just thought you seem to be in a tangle. Do you need any help?'

'Help? Oh! Yeah, right. That would be great. I've run out of nappies and I need to clean Sophie up. She's had a bit of mishap. If you could keep an eye on Ben for a minute or two, that would be great.'

'I'd be delighted,' she said, surprisingly unsurprised by the request, almost as if she had approached with this very outcome in mind. She turned towards Ben and smiled a big grey-toothed smile at him. The woman had a mouth like a neglected graveyard. 'Seems like you need some help with those sandcastles,' she said.

Ben frowned at her assessingly, staring hard at her dentistry. For an awful moment, it looked to Phil as if he was about to ask her what had happened to her teeth.

'Are those ones broken?' asked Dawn, pointing at the site of Sophie's demolition.

'Daddy said he'd help me, then he didn't,' said Ben, in his wronged-man-bravely-maintaining-his-moral-superiority voice.

'Well, I can give you a hand,' said Dawn. 'In fact, I'm quite a sandcastle expert.'

'A sandcastle expert?' said Ben, liking the sound of this term, his interest piqued sufficiently to override his horror at her bad teeth.

'Oh, yes,' said Dawn. 'You wait and see.'

'Thank you so much,' said Phil. 'This is really kind of you.'

He picked Sophie up, holding her out awkwardly from his body to try and minimise the general smearing of faeces, and carried her back to the room. At the door he glanced back, and saw Dawn and Ben forming a happy diptych. She was digging and he was chatting away happily, showing her exactly how to restore his structure to its former glory. They had already fallen naturally into their roles as foreman and labourer.

Phil stripped Sophie off outside the room and dumped the soiled clothes on the veranda. He'd deal with them later. The best way to sort out this situation was to hose her down in the bath, then start again from scratch. She wouldn't like it, but it had to be done.

By the time he had pulled this off, supporting her with one arm in the tub while splashing tepid water over her with the other, she was purple with rage and shrieking with an intensity that would have been a histrionic reaction to attempted murder. He dried her as quickly as he could, making a mental note to check the bath for flecks of shit before he next used it, then encased her safely in a dry nappy and carried her out onto the veranda. The woman was still happily navvying for Ben.

Phil called out to her, shouting over Sophie's screams, 'ARE YOU OK?'

She waved back. 'FINE! AREN'T WE, BEN?'

'WE'VE DONE *SIX*!' said Ben.

'FANTASTIC!' said Phil, not knowing or caring what they had done six of. 'SOPHIE'S A BIT UPSET. I'M GOING TO GIVE HER A BOTTLE. IS THAT OK?'

'FINE! TAKE AS LONG AS YOU LIKE!'

Phil walked back into the room with Sophie, made up a bottle, and sat on the bed, propping himself up with a generous nest of pillows. He put Sophie on his lap and gave her the bottle. She downed it quickly, and almost immediately began to fall into a post-apoplectic doze. She was lovely and warm on top of him – a delicious, happy weight. He was very cosy on the bed. And as he watched her lids getting heavier, he sensed how easy it would be for him to fall into the same state.

Really, he ought to take her back outside. Or maybe put her into the cot and lock the door, then go to relieve the woman who was looking after Ben. They were more or less within earshot. There was a baby monitor somewhere. That's what he ought to do.

But if he moved, it might wake her, and a nap at this time of day was always helpful. And he really was so comfortable, too. What would be the harm in staying put, just for a while? Ben was happy. The woman was happy. He and Sophie were certainly happy. Everyone was at peace. Why risk shattering it all just to stick to some rigid timetable? They were on holiday. Everyone was supposed to be relaxing. And for once, Phil really did feel relaxed. Relaxed and sleepy.

Just forty winks. A quick snooze, cuddling his baby. What harm could it do?

He awoke – he had no idea how much later – to the sound of his wife's voice. 'What's going on?' she said.

'Er ...' He didn't even remember falling asleep, so couldn't quite understand why he was now waking up. Looking up at her from the bed, discovering Sophie asleep in his arms, he realised he couldn't answer her question. What *was* going on? He had no idea.

'Why is there a heap of shitty clothes on the veranda?'

Ah, yes. He was beginning to remember. 'Er ... I just left them there for a minute.'

'A minute? It's completely dry and caked on. It's disgusting. You're going to have to deal with them.'

'I know.'

'Why isn't Sophie in the cot?'

'Oh, we dozed off here. Just for a second.'

Joanna stepped fully into the room and looked around the corner at Ben's bed. 'Where's Ben?'

'He's outside.'

'OUTSIDE?'

'It's fine. He's with the woman from next door.'

'You left him with the woman from next door?'

'Just for a minute. She offered. There was a nappy situation, then Sophie needed a drink, then I realised it was time for her rest ...' but he was talking to himself. Joanna had gone. She returned a few seconds later, with a look of panic and rage on her face.

'Where outside?'

'Right outside.'

'He's not there.'

'What?'

'He's not there. Where is he?'

'Outside.'

'HE'S NOT OUTSIDE, PHIL. WHERE IS HE? WHAT HAVE YOU DONE?'

'He's right there.'

Phil stood and walked out onto the veranda. Ben wasn't there. The woman wasn't there.

'WHAT HAVE YOU DONE, PHIL? WHAT THE HELL HAVE YOU DONE? I GO AWAY FOR *ONE HOUR*. ONE MEASLY HOUR.'

Phil's heart was suddenly pumping furiously.

'We can knock on their door. Maybe they went in.'

Phil knocked on the door. He knocked as hard as he could. He knocked until his knuckles hurt. There was no response.

'MY GOD, PHIL! WHAT HAVE YOU DONE? WHAT ON EARTH HAVE YOU DONE? WHAT KIND OF AN IDIOT ARE YOU?'

Phil had never seen such loathing on anyone's face as the look his wife was giving him now. Nor had he ever felt such a sudden plummet into abject fear.

'Give me the baby,' said Joanna, snatching Sophie away

from him. Clutching her hard, Joanna set off down the beach at a run, shouting.

'BEN! BEN! WHERE ARE YOU? BEN! BEN!'

Phil stared at her, frozen, rooted to the spot. He couldn't think straight, and he couldn't move his limbs. He had left Ben right there. He could see the spot. The sandcastles were still there. More of them than before. He knew the woman. They'd spoken to her, several times. They'd eaten a meal with her. She was fine. There was nothing weird about her.

'ARE YOU JUST GOING TO STAND THERE?' shouted Joanna.

'No. No,' said Phil. He forced his legs into action, and set off down the beach, in the opposite direction to Joanna. The sand was scorching underfoot. Phil began to wonder if this day was going to be the dividing line between one life, a happy life and another kind of existence altogether.

'BEN! BEN! BEN! BEN!'

He could hardly get the words out of his mouth. The blood was pounding so hard in his head that he thought he might faint.

He couldn't have gone far. Surely. The Thing You Most Fear couldn't happen to them. Not here. Surely.

Last

ALI SMITH was born in Inverness in 1962. She is the author of *Free Love* (1995), which won the Saltire First Book Award; *Like* (1997); *Other Stories and Other Stories* (1999); *Hotel World* (2001), which was short-listed for both the Orange Prize and the Booker Prize; *The Whole Stories and Other Stories* (2003); *The Accidental* (2005), which won the Whitbread Award; and *Girl Meets Boy* (2007). Her latest book is *The First Person and Other Stories* (2008). Ali Smith writes regularly for the *Guardian*, the *Scotsman* and the *TLS*. She lives in Cambridge.

I HAD COME TO THE CONCLUSION. I had nothing more to say. I had looked in the cupboard and found it was bare. I had known in my bones it was over. I had reached the end of my tether. I had dug until I'd hit rock bottom. I had gone past the point of no return. I had come to the end of the line.

But at the end of the line, when the train stopped, like everybody else I got off and walked back along the platform to the exit. I scrabbled in my pocket for the ticket, fed the ticket into the slot in the machine. The machine snatched it with what felt like volition but what was really only automation, then opened its padded gates for me and shut them behind me. Then I walked out past the taxis, across the dismal car park and up the pedestrian bridge.

From here I could see the empty train, the same train we'd all just been on, as it shunted from the platform to wherever the empty trains go. From this angle I could see into the carriages, in fact I could see right into the carriage I'd just travelled to the end of the line in.

The carriage had been packed, all the seats taken ten minutes before the train left and the train still filling with people until the moment before its doors closed on us; the journey had been an exercise in aloofness, with people who didn't know each other swaying towards then carefully away from each other in the aisles, people trying to not sway into each other in the doorways, people towering above the rather buxom woman in the wheelchair, reading the magazine. She'd been there in the special wheelchair-designated place when I boarded the train. Somehow the swaying standing people were worse above her head, I thought, than they were above the heads of people just sitting ordinarily in the train seats; somehow it was the last word in rudeness, that the edge of one man's open jacket kept brushing against the back of her head.

That's how I knew, from up here on the slant of the bridge, that this train below was the same train I'd just been on, and that's how I could spot exactly the carriage I'd been on, because that woman in the wheelchair who'd been in the same carriage as me was still there on that empty train, I could see from here that she was leaning forward in her chair and beating on the train door with her fist. I could see she was yelling. I knew she was making a lot of noise and I knew I couldn't hear any of it.

I watched the silent beat of her. Then the train slid out of view.

The driver will find her, I thought. Surely they check to make sure their trains are empty. Surely people must fall asleep or be caught on trains like that all the time. Probably she has a mobile and has called people and let them know. It's even possible that she wants to be on that train, that she's meant to be on it, there, alone.

But through the scratchy perspex of the other side of the pedestrian bridge I could see that there was a footworn footpath going down towards the rails, the kind we used to make in the riverbanks and slopes of the fields when I was a child, the kind that people make in places where paths aren't supposed to be.

At the bottom of the path the barbed wire fence that shut the station off from the public was splayed open the size of a big dog or a crouching adult. Next to this hole was a sign which said, in letters large enough for me to be able to read them from here, that trespassing was prohibited, that the only people allowed past this point were rail personnel. If we find you trespassing you will be fined.

I found I was thinking about the person, or people, who'd originally worded that sign. Had there been special meetings held to decide the wording? Did they, or he, or she, pause for a moment at all over find and fined?

And why, anyway, did the word fine mean a payment for doing something illegal at the same time as it meant everything from okay to really grand? And was it at all connected, that the word grand could also mean a thousand pounds? Did that mean that notions of fineness and grandness, in their travelling etymologies, were often tied up with notions of money? I hadn't a clue. But I had an urge to look them up in a dictionary and see. It was the first urge to do such a thing I'd had in quite a while.

I turned round. I retraced my steps down the slant of the bridge and under the little barrier between the bridge and the grassy bank, and went down the path towards the hole in the bent-back fence. I slid myself through the space without catching my clothes on any of the sharp cut-open bits of it and I stood up straight again in the litter next to the bramble bushes. I glanced one way then the other along the set of rails in front of me. A train was up ahead of me. I wondered if it was the right train. There was something fine in it, just walking along a forbidden track, thinking pointlessly about words. Travelling etymologies, that was a good phrase. It would be a good name for a rock band. It would be a good social-anthropological name for a tribe of people who jumped rolling-stock and lived on it, sheltering under waterproof tarpaulins when it rained, sitting when it was sunny on the footplate spaces, if that's what they were called, or lying stretched out on the tops of the cargoes of carriages; reprobates, meaningful dropouts, living a freer, more meaningful life than any of us others were able to choose. The Travelling Etymologies. It was a good idea, and now background-murmuring through my head again, for the first time in ages, was a welcome sound, the sound of the long thin never-ending-seeming rolling-stock of words, the sound of life and industry, word after word after word coupled to each other by tough little iron joists, travelling from the past through the present to the future like rolling stones that gather moss after all.

I mean, take a rich, full word like buxom, which was a word I knew the history of, since at another point in my life, in what felt like a life centuries earlier than this one now, I had liked words immensely and thought a lot about using them and about how they were used. At the beginning of its history buxom meant obedient, compliant, gracious. Then later in time it meant blithe, and lively, then a bit later still it started to mean overweight, because larger people are traditionally seen as blithe and cheery. Then it stopped being about both men and women and became only about women, in a revealing fusion of compliant, obedient, merry and big-breasted.

Or the word aloof, which was a shipping term, came from luff, the word for the command to distance your boat from something too dangerously close to it. Or the word clue, too, which came from the word for a ball of thread and the coinage of which was probably something to do with the big ball of string Theseus took into the labyrinth with him to mark his way out and defeat the Minotaur. Ariadne got it from Daedalus, the inventor, and she gave it to Theseus, with whom she was in love, and the ball of string saved his life and made him a hero. Then he abandoned her on Naxos island. She woke on the beach and she hadn't a clue where he'd gone, till she saw the sails of his ship disappearing over the sea's horizon. Now that's what I call aloof. I was walking the outside length of a dark, dead, switched-off train. Words were stories in themselves. Stamina was another good one, whose root and path I couldn't remember wholly but knew was something to do with the length of a person's life, the length of the life-force allotted to each of us at birth.

Strength and fragility both, something lasting and something fearfully delicate, held there in the one word, and there in front of me was the door with the woman in the wheelchair behind it, who, when she saw movement below her – I say below her because I was down on ground level, quite different from platform level and platform perspective, and could look in through the dark glass of the door and make out her ankles on the chair's fold-out footrests – knocked what she could reach of herself and her chair against the glass with such eagerness, force and determination that I knew properly for the first time in my life exactly what the word stamina meant.

Hello! I shouted up.

I saw her mouth open and close. I looked high above my head at the buttons with which we usually open the doors of trains. They were unlit, as I'd expected. I stood back in the grass so she could see me more clearly and I waved my arms about. I realised I could say anything to this person and she wouldn't be able to hear; I realised that unless she could lipread she'd not know what I was saying. I could ask her what happened to her, why and how she was in a wheelchair. I could recite the whole of 'Kubla Khan' by Coleridge, or tell her all about Theseus and Ariadne, and she'd have to listen, while not listening at all, obviously. It had the makings of the perfect relationship. I could tell her endlessly, boringly, about words and how they meant and why they mattered, and what had happened in my life to make them not matter.

Instead, what I found myself talking about was the place where my father had his workshop when I was a child, and how it had been at the back of the railway, so that I had spent a lot of my holiday hours in the grassy banks alongside sets of rails much like where we were now.

It's been bulldozed, years ago, I said to the woman behind the glass doors. There's a furniture warehouse on it now, it's a shopping mall and a station car park where the old workshops were. It was a kind of nowhere, a nowhere before the new nowheres that shopping malls are now. It was quite a special place. The grass there was thick with clover, presumably it still is, if there's any grassy space there that still goes straight down to the earth. Finding four-leafed clovers there was pretty mundane. We found five- and six- and seven-leafed clovers there too, and once an eight. I put what I found in a book. I've no idea which book. They must still be somewhere on the shelves in the house, folded flat in there with their ridged green leaves arranged so you could see how many. I wonder if I'd find any if I were to go home and look for them tonight. Needle in a haystack. Clover in a shut book.

When I finished speaking the woman behind the doors began saying something impatient-looking. But listening for what I couldn't hear had made my ears different. Now I could hear birds, air, the traffic in the distance. Then what I could hear most clearly was unexpected music.

Three boys were coming along the path I thought of as my path now, along the side of the train. One had a ghetto blaster. A black dog with his lead trailing on the ground was ahead of them, stopping to sniff the grass and stones, then loping off in front again when the boys got ahead instead. The dog saw me and stopped. The boys stopped. They were all in clothes that looked too big for them. The dog was streamlined in comparison, held in one neat piece by his skin. They backed up two or three steps as if they were all part of the same single body. Then they shrugged apart and came forward again, because I was no threat to anyone.

Trespassing's illegal, one of the boys said to me when they were close enough.

I said nothing. I pointed to the woman in the train.

She's got wheels, man, the smallest boy said to the others.

All three waved to the woman. She waved back. One boy held up a packet of cigarettes. The woman nodded and shouted the silent word yes. The boy with the ghetto blaster turned the volume off.

Can't hear you, he shouted.

The woman mouthed the word yes again, with finesse, as if very quietly. The boy with the cigarette packet opened the packet, took out two cigarettes and threw them both at the shut door. Somehow it was funnier because he threw two cigarettes, not just one. The woman held up her hand as if to say, wait a minute. She put her other hand in a bag on the side of the chair and took out an umbrella with a hooked handle. Then she backed her chair away from the door. She wheeled herself into the carriage, lined up the wheelchair next to the train seats and, using all the strength in her arms, she lifted and shifted herself from the wheelchair onto the seat. She got her breath back. She bent her head over the umbrella, lengthened the umbrella somehow, then she reached with the lengthened umbrella to hook open the little train window above her.

The boys cheered. I did too. Now we could hear the woman's voice through the open window. She said in a voice that was proper, rather upper middle class, that she wished she'd thought how to open that window earlier, and that she would love a cigarette, that she hadn't had a cigarette for over five years now, that she deserved one after today. She thanked the boys. She turned then and said a separate hello to me, as if we were all at a party she'd thrown and she was simply emphasising how very pleased she was to see each and every one of us.

I saw you on the train looking so thoughtful, she said. Thank you for finding me.

The notion that I had been seen, and that from the outside I had at some unknowing point looked thoughtful, made me feel strange, better. The idea that I had found anything filled me with wonder. As the boys took turns trying to throw single cigarettes up in the air and through the open window, I felt myself become substantial. Now the boys were scrabbling about on the ground trying to find the fallen cigarettes, arguing about picking the cigarettes up off the ground and not crushing them. They shouted with happiness when one went through the high window and landed on the woman's lap. They argued about whose aim was truest, who would be best to throw the little red plastic lighter.

Inside the train the woman waved her hands to get their attention.

She tossed the cigarette up at her mouth and caught it wrong way round, like a minor circus trick. The three boys shouted their admiration. She took the cigarette out of her mouth, put it the right way round, then got herself ready to catch the lighter, which she did, with one hand. She lit her cigarette. The tallest, the shyest of the three, tapped on the sealed window with the stick he was carrying and pointed it at the No Smoking logo. He blushed at the way his friends laughed, the way the woman laughed behind the window, the way I was laughing too.

I stood directly under the open window and shouted up through it that I was off to find someone to unlock the train and let her out.

The smallest boy snorted a laugh.

Don't need to go nowhere, he said. We'll get your friend out.

All three boys stood back from the train carriage. The smallest scouted about for a pebble. The other two bent down and picked up large stones. The dog started to bark. It was almost immediately after they started to throw the stones at the side of the train that the men in the luminous waistcoats came running towards us.

Shortly after this the afternoon came to an end. We said our goodbyes. We went our different ways. I myself went back to the station and bought a ticket home. What was it you were telling me down there? the woman asked me when she'd finally got off the train, after they'd backed it to a plat-form, opened its doors, brought the sloping ramp they use to help people in wheelchairs to get on and off and allowed her to wheel herself out. There were many apologies from people in suits and uniform. Well, that's the last time I take the train! is what she said, with some campness and a great deal of panache, when the doors finally automatically hissed open on her, centre stage, like the curtains of a strange tiny theatre. The people on the plaform laughed politely. She didn't mean it, of course she didn't.

In Shakespeare, the word stone can also mean a mirror.

The word pebble has, in its time, also meant a lens made of rock crystal and a sizeable amount of gunpowder.

The word mundane comes from *mundus*, the Latin word for the world.

At one time the word cheer seems to have meant the human face.

The word last is a very versatile word. Among other more unexpected things – like the piece of metal shaped like a foot which a cobbler uses to make shoes – it can mean both finality and continuance, it can mean the last time and something a lot more lasting than that.

To conclude once held the meaning to enclose.

To tell has at different times meant the following: to express in words, to narrate, to explain, to calculate, to count, to order, to give away secrets, to say goodbye.

To live in clover means to live luxuriously, in abundance.

Long Time, No See

AUTHOR'S NOTE

In 1998, between what are formally acknowledged as my sixth and seventh novels (*Double Fault* and *We Need to Talk About Kevin*), I completed novel #6.5. *The New Republic* has never been published. Because its subject matter concerns terrorism, I feared that after 9/11 the novel had been, as they say, 'overtaken by events'. I had imagined that if I ever did publish TNR, it would have to be substantially reworked. I have changed my mind. As we draw away from 9/11, it is worth remembering how both Britain and America regarded terrorism – in particular, IRA terrorism – previous to that watershed in 2001. Which is to say, parties in both countries fell all over themselves to excuse it.

Set in a historically fictional mid-1990s, *The New Republic* is not simply about terrorism, a non-fiction concern, but more primarily about the mystery of charisma, a subject that has engaged me for many years. Oh, and don't worry – as I would – that this novel is all about Northern Ireland. It concerns instead a mythical and to my mind far more entertaining outfit called Os Soldatos Ousados de Barba ('The Daring Soldiers of Barba'), or the SOB. Barba is a fictional peninsula of Portugal that I drew onto the map with my rapidograph. This is Chapter 3, titled as a stand-alone story, 'Long Time, No See'.

LIONEL SHRIVER was born in North Carolina in 1957. She has lived in Nairobi, Bangkok and Belfast, and currently lives in London. Her seventh novel, *We Need to Talk About Kevin*, won the 2005 Orange Prize. Her other novels are: *Double Fault*, *A Perfectly Good Family*, *Game Control*, *Ordinary Decent Criminals*, *Checker and the Derailleurs*, *The Female of the Species* and, most recently, *The Post-Birthday World*. Her new novel, *Time Is Money*, will be published in Spring 2010.

IT HAD BEEN ALMOST TWENTY YEARS since they'd nodded stiffly at each other across a throng of parents at Yardley Prep's graduation in Connecticut. Still, Edgar didn't anticipate having any trouble recognising Toby Falconer when they met for a drink. Falconer was one of those golden boys. No doubt every high school had one, although the singular was incongruous as a type; presumptively there was no-one else like him.

A Falconer managed to be the centre of attention when he wasn't even there. He always got girls, but more to the point he got *the girl*. Whichever dish you yourself conjured with the bathroom door closed, she'd be smitten with our hero instead. Some cachet would rub off, of course, but if you hung with a Falconer you'd spend most of your dates fielding questions about his troubled childhood. A Falconer's liberty was almost perfectly unfettered, because he was never punished for his sins. Anyway, a Falconer's sins wouldn't seem depraved but merely naughty, waggish, or rather enchanting really, part of the package without which a Falconer wouldn't be the endearing rogue whom we know and love and infinitely forgive. Besides, who would risk his displeasure by bringing him to book? He did everything with flare, not only because he was socially adroit, but because the definition of flare in his circle was however the Falconer did whatever the Falconer did. To what extent a Falconer's magnetism could be ascribed to physical beauty was impossible to determine. Good looks couldn't have hurt; but if a Falconer had any deviant feature – a lumpy nose, a single continuous eyebrow, feminine lips – that feature would simply serve to reconfigure the beautiful as archetype. A Falconer set the standard, so by his very nature could not appear unattractive, make a plainly stupid remark or do anything awkward at which others would laugh, save in an ardent, collusive or sycophantic spirit.

Hitherto Edgar Kellogg had been the Falconer's counterpart, that symbiotic creature without which a Falconer could not exist. The much-admired required the admirer, and to his own dismay Edgar had more than once applied for the position. In fact, Edgar's public manner – gruff, tough, wary and deadpan – was wildly discrepant with his secret weakness for becoming captivated by passing Falconers, and he worried privately that the whole purpose of his crusty exterior was to contain an inside full of goo. He couldn't bear to conceive of himself as a sidekick. Having ever been slavishly enthralled shamed him almost as much as having once been fat. Hence of Edgar's several ambitions at thirty-seven the most dominant among them was never to succumb to the enchantment of a Falconer again.

To date, the only weapon that had overthrown a Falconer's tyranny was cruel, disciplined disillusionment. Sometimes a Falconer turned out to be a fraud. Lo and behold he could be clumsy, if you kept watch. At length it proved thoroughly possible, if you forced yourself, to laugh at his foibles in a fashion that was less than flattering. Wising up was painful at first, but a relief, and when all was said and done Edgar would be lonely but free. Yet taking the anointed down a peg or two was a puzzling, even depressing exercise, in consequence of which he reserved his most scathing denunciations for the very people with whom he had once been most powerfully entranced.

Edgar's feelings about Falconer at Yardley Prep had been so perfectly ambivalent that they divided with the one-for-you-and-one-for-me precision of a child splitting jellybeans. Freshman and sophomore years he'd half-adored and half-detested Falconer from afar, junior year he'd half-adored and half-detested Falconer up close, and senior year he'd half-adored and half-detested Falconer from afar again. While continuing to maintain the same precarious balance of mixed emotions, denied the mesmerising daily spectacle of Falconer gliding with otherworldly nonchalance down the hall, in adulthood Edgar had settled until this very afternoon on half-adoring and half-detesting his icon-cum-nemesis from a safe distance.

Falconer's fortunes had been easy to follow. A foreign correspondent for the *National Record*, he filed peripatetically from Beirut to Belfast to Baghdad. Never from anywhere placid, that was for sure. Man, that was the life. While Edgar learned to his despair how little money was worth if it couldn't buy you out of slogging into a New York law firm at 7 a.m., he'd often grabbed the *National Record* in the Equitable Building's lobby, but refused to take the plunge and subscribe. Though the sole reason he bought the rag was to search out Toby's byline, whenever he located one of Falconer's stories he couldn't bring himself to read beyond the lead. Whether he was afraid the article would be sensational or substandard he'd never identified, since Edgar was an era throwback for whom self-examination seemed as pragmatically useful as learning Sanskrit.

Accordingly, when earlier this year Edgar had ditched a 'promising' career in corporate law (though what it promised, of course, was more corporate law) in order to try his own hand at journalism, he was reluctant to question to what degree this rash and so far financially disastrous professional U-turn had been influenced by Toby Falconer – who had always obtained the funnier friends, the prettier girls, the sexier summer jobs, and for the last twelve years the far jazzier vocation. Frankly, the real reason lawyers were compensated so lavishly was that they were paid to attend to the most stultifying aspects of modern life; they were paid well the way garbage collectors really ought to be paid well, or sewage workers. Moreover, the chances of distinguishing himself as yet one more New York attorney were negligible. If Toby Falconer and Edgar Kellogg were both drawn to journalism, maybe this merely indicated that the two boys had had more in common at Yardley than Edgar had ever dared believe possible as a kid.

He was a little surprised that Falconer's choice of venue for their reunion didn't show more panache. The Red Shoe had once been a chic Flatiron watering hole, but that was years back. Since, the crimson velvet cushions had faded to sickly pink, their plush nap flattened like a cat's in the sink. The varnish on the dark banquettes had worn to expose stained pine. Its waiters were old enough to no longer describe their shifts as 'day-jobs'. Even from his pink-granite sarcophagus uptown, Edgar had clued up that The Red Shoe was déclassé. Perhaps it was sufficiently out of fashion to qualify for a tongue-in-cheek reprise, and Toby, as usual, was setting the pace.

Edgar paused in The Red Shoe's foyer, preparing himself for his old friend – or whatever it was that Toby had become by senior year. After mussing his hair, unbuttoning his vest, and yanking the Windsor knot to the side the way he'd always wrenched his school tie, Edgar ditched his suit jacket on the coat rack. Even after he'd shed his old tub-o'-guts tag, his image at Yardley was hostile, unkempt, and seditious; an intact three-piece might give Falconer a shock.

Edgar turned and heard a plop. The hanger arm had flipped upside down and dumped his jacket on the floor. Stripped screw. Flustered, Edgar scooped up the jacket, hastily brushing the lapels. Damn. Especially in these inbetween moments – tossing a coat on a rack, swinging from a bucket seat – Toby Falconer had been infuriatingly graceful.

Inhaling, Edgar launched through the double-doors, his coat hooked over a shoulder. He was flattering himself to picture his old high school buddy, waiting expectantly in a corner by himself. Falconer was always mobbed. So just locate the social goat-fuck in the very centre of this dive, its biggest table, the one crammed with extra chairs – one more of which Edgar would be obliged to fetch and wedge in somewhere. Falconer would be braying, those mighty fluoride-fortified teeth arrayed to the smoky tin ceiling, arms spread and palms lifted like Jesus, the rest of the rabble wheezing, flopping, wiping tears.

But the bar was quiet.

Edgar scanned the large round middle tables for that beacon of hair, so blond it was almost white. It was unlikely that

Falconer had kept that smooth narrow chest into manhood, but the guy had been vain enough at sixteen that he'd probably become one of those Nautilus obsessives who poured rice milk on his muesli. Besides, Edgar's paltry efforts to update his mental mock-up of Toby Falconer – to bulge the muscular wavelets of his stomach into a paunchy swell, to dull the sublime adolescent promise of that platinum blond down to pewter – felt juvenile, like drawing zits on a *New York Times Magazine* model with a ballpoint.

No beacon. Just one subdued party, workmates, glancing at watches, looking for an excuse to scram. A couple of loners sagged in booths – one rung-out dishrag, quietly sobbing (that made three crying women that he'd happened across today; the daily New York average was five or six), and some balding nondescript.

But then, why would Toby Falconer be prompt? Edgar would stew here for an hour, knocking back beers and refurbishing a resentment that two decades had failed to anodise into indifference. Finally when Edgar was requesting his check, Toby would sashay in, double doors swinging with his dozen disciples, all drunk, loud and dashingly dressed, at last infusing this old man's bathrobe of a pub with its original camp, smoking-jacket flash. For now refusing to consider the higher likelihood that Falconer had blown off their appointment altogether, Edgar assumed a chair at the middle-most table and signalled for a waiter.

'Kellogg?'

Edgar twisted at the finger on his arm, and experienced one of those blank moments induced by headlines about Montenegro. It was the balding nondescript. His eyes were mild and dilute, their lids puffy; his face was broad and bland, his figure padded. The man's skin was pallid, in contrast to the lustrous walnut glow of a thrill-seeker who hot-dogged the winter slopes and sailed at the head of his regatta. Yet between the grey straggles across his scalp gleamed a few nostalgic streaks of platinum.

'Falconer!' Edgar pumped the stranger's hand.

'I don't know what football team you're expecting. Let's sit over here. Listen, I'm sorry about The Red Shoe. Last time I was here it was hopping, but I don't get out much. Christ, you look the same! A little more pissed off, maybe … If that's possible. But you sure kept that weight off.'

'You, too, you look – terrific!'

Falconer guffawed, a more muffled version of the old clarion bray, recognisable but rounder, less piercing. 'Never thought I'd see the day that Edgar Kellogg was polite. I look like dogshit! Dogshit with three hyperactive kids and a depressive wife. What'll you have?'

Edgar liked to think of himself as a Wild Turkey man. 'Amstel Light.'

'Never lose *the fear*, do you?' Falconer smiled, his teeth no longer blinding, though that was unfair; everybody's teeth yellowed a bit with age. But the smile also seemed physically smaller, which was impossible.

'Not quite,' Edgar admitted, telling himself not to stare. 'Inside this runt is always a lard-bucket struggling to get out.'

'A lot of Yardley's a blur for me now, but the one thing I remember clear as a *Dialing for Dollars* re-run is our very own Incredible Shrinking Man – Edgar Kellogg, dropping a size a week. I could track the calendar by the notches cinched on your belt. Night after night in the dining hall, chomping through a barricade of celery sticks. Amazing.'

'I'd read somewhere that you burn more calories eating celery than you ingest. Still, I don't remember inspiring much awe. More like hilarity.'

'Only for the first fifty pounds.'

'Fifty pounds' worth of ridicule could last a lifetime.'

'Seems so. Look at you. You're still mad!'

Edgar exhaled a derisive *puh* and looked away, signalling once more, fruitlessly, for the waiter. He cracked a half-smile, and tore at a cuticle. 'Maybe.'

Toby biffed him softly on the arm. 'You knocked my socks off. Never seen such determination, before or since.'

'Yeah, I did get the feeling at the time that's what earned me—'

'Earned you what?'

'Admission. To your—' it was hard to put this tactfully, 'exclusive circle.'

'I don't remember *admitting* you to anything,' Toby said dismissively. 'You just stopped keeping to yourself for a while. A short while, come to think of it. ... Service stinks here. Better get us drinks from the bar.'

Edgar welcomed the interruption, since Falconer's rewrite of history was outlandish.

Accepting his Amstel, he tried to restore an easy humour. 'I've no idea how I'll ever get to be a larger-than-life character drinking candy-ass beer.'

'You're a character.' Falconer reared back in the booth with some of his old Yardley authority and took a slug of his microbrew draught. 'That's enough. No such thing as larger-than-life, Kellogg. There's only life-size, and any magnification is just other people's bullshit ... So listen, how'd the interview go?'

Still dazed by his good luck, only now did Edgar apprehend that the job interview from which he'd just come had gone staggeringly well. He'd have liked to conclude that he therefore cut an impressive figure. It was more likely that Falconer had given him a recommendation much more enthusiastic than his virtual-stranger status merited, and that Falconer had stroke. 'Swell, I guess. Your editor gave me a string. In Barba.'

Toby made a face. 'I should have warned you that's what he had in mind. Better than nothing, I hope. But I've done a couple of features out of Barba. It ain't Club Med.'

'You think it's dangerous?' asked Edgar hopefully.

'Well, as you know the SOB has never set off a bomb in their own territory. I guess the logic runs, don't shit in your own bed. But that could change. And what makes for a dangerous place is dangerous people. Or that's the line Saddler used to squeeze a hardship allowance out of Wallasek. I don't know why his lordship bothered to be so creative. Guy Wallasek would have handed Saddler his first-born son, no questions asked.'

Much to Edgar's astonishment – with his dismal clip-file of in-flight magazine stories padded with old law review articles, he'd hoped for no better than the go-ahead to submit the odd op-ed – Falconer's editor at the *National Record* had suggested earlier that afternoon that he fill in for some pretentious-sounding character called Barrington Saddler, another foreign correspondent, who had melodramatically disappeared. The name had put Edgar off from the start. 'Saddler' was burdensome, mounting. The 'Barrington' bit was overblown and beefy, and anyone who didn't have the wit to shorten the affected appellation down to 'Barry' was a pompous ass.

If the likes of Toby Falconer, or the old Falconer at least, was indeed a type, sight-unseen this Saddler person belonged to the very same Exception To Every Rule set. Simply put, they were the sort of folks about whom other folks couldn't stop talking. As if to illustrate this thumb-nail definition, the portly Wallasek – so wise-yet-weary and gruff-yet-fatherly as to suggest that he'd been taking Big City Editor lessons – had spent five minutes describ-ing Edgar's new job and forty-five describing the vanished reporter's devastated girlfriends. (Abruptly going missing – well, that was just the sort of stunt these people pulled.) In kind, Toby's reference to Barrington Saddler immedi-ately set Edgar lurching between those familiar poles of re-pulsion and attraction; thrown queasily between opposing inclinations, he might have been churning up switchbacks in a bus. He both wanted to talk about this preposterous fellow, greedily, and wanted to avoid all mention of the man with equal desperation. When he gave in and pursued the subject, he instantly regretted it, the way you curse yourself for having picked at a scab. '*What* is so fucking wonderful about the little prick?'

'Saddler's not little. I've only met him a handful of times. Bit scary, frankly.'

Even in this bafflingly modest incarnation, Edgar couldn't fathom Tobias Falconer being frightened by any-body. 'That name for starters. What kind of a blowhard goes by "Barrington"?'

'You clearly haven't met the guy. Weird, but it suits him. He's English, you know. And large. He almost requires three syllables.'

'So he's *fat*,' Edgar concluded victoriously.

Falconer frowned. 'Nnno-o. Just big. Big, big, big. In every sense.'

'Why "scary"? I get the impression you don't like the guy much.'

'That's just it: I shouldn't. He's got my own editor wrapped around his pinky. He gets away with murder – like, for 0.01 percent of the shit he's pulled any mere mortal would have been sacked. He has this tut-tut, frightfully-frightfully accent that makes Americans feel crass and Coca-Cola by comparison. So whenever I've thought about it – and I've thought about it, which is one thing that's scary – everything about the man grates. But Saddler only gets on my nerves when he's out of the room. He never rubs me the wrong way in person. Face-to-face Barrington Saddler is inexpressibly charming, and I spend the entire time frantically trying to get *him* to like *me*.'

'*That* is scary,' said Edgar, thinking: money down, no-one had ever described Edgar Kellogg behind his back as 'inexpressibly charming'.

'How'd you find Wallasek?' asked Falconer.

'Paternalistic for my taste.' Absent any encouragement in Toby's expression, Edgar exercised his proclivity for putting his foot in it. 'And awfully *in the know*. Wallasek thinks he has a window into the mind of terrorists because of Saddler – when what are the chances that both of them know dick? Also,' Edgar plunged recklessly on, 'Wallasek talks a humble line about journalists being "history's secretaries", but you can tell he thinks journalism is a lofty calling fraught with daunting tests of fire. As opposed to being mostly about the ability to write a sentence. Which I can, but I don't think he was impressed by my clips. I've only been at this a few months, and Wallasek didn't care what the articles said – typical name-brand mentality. I didn't walk in with the *New York Times* and the *Atlantic* plastered to my forehead ... What's so funny?'

'You really haven't changed, have you?'

'How's that?' asked Edgar warily.

'Guy Wallasek gave you an interview on the basis of a pretty slight clip-file, and what's more gave you a job. Which, though Barba's not Hawaii, I assume you want.'

'So?'

'Doesn't that make you grateful?'

Edgar folded his arms and bunched into the corner, scowling to beat the band. It was a hatches-battened position he'd often assumed when he was fat. 'Wallasek offered me a temporary post that could be whipped out from under me by your big, big, big friend any time he cares to show his face, an arrangement that would be intolerable to staffers. A string will pay squat. I was a sharp lawyer and I can write. I'll do an ace job, and he's getting a bargain. Why should I be grateful?'

Falconer shook his head. 'So hard on people, Kellogg. You that hard on yourself?'

An honest answer was too complicated – that he hacked on other people as a substitute for hacking on himself, and the displacement didn't work. A simpler answer – that Edgar perceived himself as an island of underrated promise in a sea of undeserving incompetence – would sound iffy in the open air. 'I call them as I see them. You said yourself that Wallasek's relationship to this Barrington guy is fucked up.'

'I didn't say that. Wallasek's a good editor, and a decent man. He claims he doesn't, but he misses the fray – being so smack in the middle when some corner of the world goes up in flames that the hairs singe off your arm. So he has a weakness for the inside track; any journalist does. As for Saddler? Wallasek nine-to-fives it, he's bored, feels left out. Saddler blasts into town and they go out until all hours and get slammed and meet kooky people and get kicked out of bars and Wallasek feels plugged in again. A minor failing, if a failing at all. Why not give him a chance? It's not a bad policy. You're a smart guy, Kellogg, but you can be so – savage.'

Edgar felt chastened. He didn't like feeling chastened. 'Christ, Falconer. You've gone and got sincere on me.'

Toby was rolling the bottom of his empty beer mug in contemplative circles. 'I was surprised to hear from you. Not sorry. But surprised.'

Edgar wasn't about to admit that he'd rung Falconer over his own dead body; that it was only his horror at watching his nominal savings from law dwindle to nothing while he 'freelanced' that had forced him to the phone. For years, Falconer's disembodied byline in the *National Record* had given Edgar a jolt. Its AC/DC of envy and wistfulness were confusing but addictive, inspiring him to purchase what was otherwise a dull newspaper. Though having thus remained current in Edgar's life, Falconer must have long ago mothballed Edgar Kellogg. He'd only dared to call Falconer after six months of terse no-thanks e-mails from the *New Republic* and the *New Yorker*, or more often than not no reply at all, and the night-sweats had begun. In his dreams, Edgar implored Lee & Thole's senior partner to take him back without health coverage while wearing nothing but lime green socks; his old boss scolded that the firm had gone casual on Fridays but it was Thursday and his socks ought really to be brown or black. In Edgar's new trade, 'freelance' was apparently a synonym for 'unemployed', and when he used the word to acquaintances on the street they smirked.

'It has been a long time,' Edgar submitted neutrally.

Falconer laughed. 'It's been nineteen years! And when I finally hear from you, it's not because you want to invite me to your wedding, or talk about old times; you want a favour! That takes balls, boyo.'

Not wanting to question his good luck, Edgar hadn't until now confronted the improbability of Falconer having returned his out-of-the-blue call at all, much less having been so encouraging about Edgar's arguably foolhardy change of careers and eager to help. Most hacks would see Edgar as a wet-nosed neophyte, his designs on their vocation impertinent. The uncanny cordiality should have been a red flag: this was not the Toby Falconer of yore.

'Didn't beat around the bush, either,' Falconer recalled wryly. 'No small-talk.'

Edgar squirmed. 'I hate that how're-the-kids shit. No offence, but why should I care if your youngest is in the choir? You'd clue that I was hitting you up for a contact soon enough.'

'Since Yardley, I haven't even been on your Christmas card list. Weren't you worried I'd brush you off?'

'Worried? I expected it. But I figured, what's to lose? A little pride. Maybe when I was still raking in the bucks at Lee & Thole, losing face would have seemed like a big deal. In my newly influential career as a commentator on world affairs,

I've sold my car, let my health club membership lapse, and forgone the firm's box at Shea.' Edgar tossed off, 'What's next? Like any other luxury, dignity is expendable.'

Falconer shot a wry glance at Edgar's wrist. 'I see you'll sell off your dignity before you'll pawn your watch.'

Parting with the $1500 diving watch would have amounted to the ultimate admission of defeat. 'A present for passing the bar, from my mother. Call me a sap.'

'Sentimentality from you, Kellogg, is a relief. Tell you what,' Falconer continued good-naturedly, 'I'd never have given you the thumbs-up with Wallasek if I didn't expect you were capable. The one thing you were at Yardley was smart, even if I wasn't always thrilled about what you applied your intelligence to – like, to figuring out people's weak spots. Anyway, I admit I had an agenda. I've got some curiosity to satisfy. If I snagged you an interview with my editor, I had a hunch that even the surly Edgar Kellogg would feel beholden enough to have this drink.'

Edgar sat up in surprise. 'I wasn't sure you'd remember me.'

'How could I forget? Some of the things you said about me senior year. They got back. Maybe they were meant to.'

Edgar had contempt for New Age confessionalism, and wasn't going to enjoy this. He shrugged. 'Kids can be mean.'

'You're not a kid. You're still—'

'You think *I'm* mean? That's rich.'

They looked at one another squarely for a beat. 'I don't get it,' said Falconer.

'How do you think I was treated, as a two-hundred-and-forty-pound punching bag?'

'You ever going to let that go? And I thought junior year at least we treated you all right.'

'Like with Wallasek. I'm supposed to be grateful.'

Falconer threw up his hands. 'It's just – what happened? One minute you were hanging out with us twenty-four/seven, and the next, bang, opposite side of the dining hall. You passed me in in hallways like a parking sign. And then all this stuff starts filtering back, that I'm on a "power-trip", that I'm a fag, that I got other guys to write my papers—'

'You did!'

'We all did! And that I *dyed my hair*.'

'I never said that.'

'You might as well have! What got into you?'

'I liked you,' Edgar said with difficulty. 'I was disappointed.'

'I don't—'

'I overheard you, okay?' Edgar's raised voice carried over the lifeless bar and drew a glance from the sniffling Miss Lonelyhearts, who looked relieved that other people had troubles, too. 'I overheard you,' he continued quietly. 'In the locker room, you and that crowd, you didn't realise I was in the shower. I turned off the water and stayed behind the wall. I hadn't been aware that my nickname was *Special K*—'

'Come on, we were always razzing somebody—'

'This was different! You mimicked me, like, *Oh, no, I can't have that chocolate chip, it has a whole eleven calories! Or, Keep that lettuce leaf away from me! A moment on the lips, a lifetime on the hips!*' Edgar twisted in his seat. 'And you made fun of my stretch marks.'

'Edgar, that's just the way it was, and if anything a little teasing only meant you were included. It was the zeros we *didn't* talk about who you should have felt sorry for.'

Edgar looked up sharply; this was the Toby Falconer he remembered. 'It got worse. You said I was always hanging around you with goo-goo eyes. That it was like having some girl on your hands, or a lost puppy. That every time you turned around I was yapping at your heels – wanting to know where you were going so I could go too, or what club you were joining so I could join too, and what albums you liked so I could go out and buy them. You all cackled at how I'd started wearing a red baseball jacket just like yours, and how I'd applied to switch into your English section. "Clingy". You used the word "clingy". So I let go.'

Thumbs pressed into his temples, Falconer kneaded his forehead with his fingertips, eyes closed. 'God, Kellogg, I'm so sorry. I swear, it wasn't you, or only you. It was all of them. I was tired. I was only seventeen years old, and I was already tired.'

Having held in that story for two decades like a breath, now that he'd exhaled it Edgar relaxed, and looked on his companion with uncharacteristic tenderness. 'Hey, water under the bridge. Anyway, you've changed. I mean, you've grown up and all, and you seem a lot more – forgiving.' Edgar thought that was a kinder way of putting the fact that Falconer had no edge any more and had turned into a soft touch for the likes of Wallasek. 'But there's something else. Something, I don't know – missing.'

Falconer didn't take offence, but smiled wanly and smoothed his palms down his face to rest them flat on the table. 'You mean I'm not surrounded by adoring fans? I'm not tap-dancing on the table with a hat-rack?'

Edgar tore a wet shred slowly off his Amstel label. 'Whatever.'

'Senior year – you heard my father died?'

'Second-hand.'

'You weren't speaking to me at the time. Anyway, it hit me hard. All the gang were consoling, for about five minutes. Maybe that made me lucky. Maybe less, well, less prominent kids whose parents died got consoled for two or three minutes. But after my five minutes were over I was supposed to go back to thinking up pranks to play on our Spanish teacher, leading sneaks off campus after curfew, and inventing new ways to propel our pineapple upside-down cake at lunch. I couldn't do it. I had more "friends" than anyone at Yardley and I was so lonely I could scream. They all wanted their emcee back, but meanwhile, who was going to lighten things up for me?

'So my mom was a mess without my dad, and I felt bad for being away at school. My sister had started sleeping around at the age of twelve. You were spreading rumours that I led circle-jerks, and I was badgered by volunteers who wanted to join in. I was depressed and couldn't concentrate on exams. All I got from my buddies was *snap out of it*. I was sick of the phone ringing in my hall and it was always for me. I was sick of people whispering and all their little theories about what made me tick. I was sick of brown-nosers who liked me a whole lot more than I liked them.

'This is going to sound a little out there, so cut me some slack. That "something missing" you mentioned: it was all that crowd wanted and it had nothing to do with me. It was some weird power that wasn't to my credit because I didn't invent it, and it was totally beyond my comprehension. I had no idea why if I said jump in the lake, you guys would jump in the lake. If you told *me* to jump, *I* wouldn't do it. I looked at myself, I saw a regular high school senior with problems, and you people saw, what – truth is, I have no idea what you saw. This gift, it was like a magic lantern, or a mirror ball. But it was also a curse.

'So I tossed it. I didn't apply to Yale or Harvard, but Haverford. At college I wore pastel button-downs and plain slacks. I didn't talk in class, and I didn't go to keg parties. I stayed in my dorm room and studied. I was a bore, and nobody ever talked about me behind my back any more than they'd mention the wallpaper.'

'And then you lost your hair.' Edgar was being undiplomatic again, but he almost wondered if Toby's metallic locks had been yanked as punishment. The notion of willingly giving up what Falconer had in high school was obscene. If nothing else, why hadn't Toby tossed the glittering facility to Edgar?

'Like Samson.' Toby grinned. 'I wonder if it's just as well. Maybe it all came down to my hair to begin with, huh? My sister has the same colouring, and I swear that half her admirers only wanted to sink their fingers into that waist-long corn-silk. Deborah got so pissed off with one guy that she cut it off and gave it to him in a box.'

'It wasn't the hair.'

'I don't even care. Whatever you guys were so hot for, I couldn't see it myself. I'm sorry I called you "clingy". I don't remember saying it, but I'm not surprised I did. Honestly,

Kellogg, you did get to be a pain. You were always dogging me, but never wanted to really talk. That part of you I was drawn to, that lost a hundred pounds in six months? That part never seemed to speak up. And on the one hand you acted so hard-ass, but on the other you, I don't know, seemed to idolise me or something. Made me feel creepy, like a fake. I'd no idea what you saw in me, what about me was so great.'

'I guess I did try to impress you,' Edgar admitted. 'Maybe I tried too hard. But you had such style, Falconer.' Edgar couldn't help the past tense. 'It's rare.'

'I may be kidding myself that I gave it up,' Toby mused. 'It could have just got away from me.'

'I've watched out for your byline for years: from Somalia, Kosovo. I always pictured your life as racy. One reason I quit law. Thought I'd join you.'

That sentence got out before Edgar realised that it sounded like more of the same: searching a dozen Manhattan retro-chic shops for a Fifties baseball jacket, and the one that fit the best and had the coolest logo on the back just happened to be the same cardinal red as Toby Falconer's. Edgar's biggest concern about his own character was that he wasn't original. He didn't know how to become original except by imitating other people who were.

'I do my job, and pretty well,' said Falconer. 'It's more ordinary than it seems, though; workaday. I am anyway. I'm quiet. I've got to the point I don't much like being on the road, and I've encouraged Guy to give the fire-fighting assignments to younger reporters who're still hot to trot. I like going home to Linda, sourdough pretzels, and the Yankees on TV. Like you said, I'm sincere. I don't have a lot of friends, but they're real.'

Edgar raised his empty Amstel and clinked it against Falconer's mug. 'Just got yourself one more, then.' Edgar's inability to complete the toast with a swig seemed apt. If idolatry made a poor basis for a friendship, pity wasn't much of an improvement. Falconer seemed like a dead nice guy, and Edgar felt robbed.

'When you off to Barba?'

'Soon as I can pack.'

'Good luck with Saddler, anyway.'

'I don't expect to have good or bad luck with Saddler,' Edgar protested. 'He disappeared, remember? Poof. Hell, the guy probably just fell in a ditch.'

'The likes of Saddler don't just fall in ditches. Or if they do, there's a lot more to the story, and nine times out of ten they crawl out again. I got a gut sense says the legendary Barrington Saddler belongs in your life.'

Though on an official level Edgar regarded the prospect as odious, he found himself obscurely cheered up. Much as he might detest some bombastic and unaccountably fawned-over scoundrel bursting unannounced through his front door, suddenly he felt he had a future, and its vista widened into the *big, big, big* – big as life; bigger, even. As Falconer settled the bill at the bar, having waved off a half-heartedly proffered ten-spot, Edgar studied the plain, kindly face, searching its prematurely haggard lines scored by 'three hyperactive kids and a depressive wife', too many red-eyes out of Addis and tight connections in Rome. Though he thought he was scanning for some flicker of the sly, playful Adonis he'd ogled at Yardley, Edgar realised in his failure to see any resemblance at all that he didn't want to.

Out on the street, they shook hands, and Edgar added a hearty shoulder clap for good measure. Neither made a feint at arranging to meet again. 'Take care of yourself, Falconer,' Edgar said.

'Watch your back, Kellogg.'

Shaking his head, instead Edgar watched Toby Falconer's back. In no time the beige knit shirt and grey slacks blended with other pedestrians, helping to form the backdrop against which strange or striking New Yorkers would stand out.

Dog Days

JEANETTE WINTERSON was born in Manchester, England, and adopted by Pentecostal parents who brought her up in the nearby mill-town of Accrington – the background to her first novel, *Oranges Are Not the Only Fruit* (1985). After the success of that book and *The Passion* (1987), she became a full-time writer, publishing *Sexing The Cherry* (1989), *Written on the Body* (1992), *Art & Lies* (1994), *Art Objects* (essays, 1995), *Gut Symmetries* (1997), *The World and Other Places* (short stories, 1998), *The.Powerbook* (2000), *Lighthousekeeping* (2004), and her latest, *The Stone Gods* (2007). She has written four books for children: *The King of Capri* (2003), *Tanglewreck* (2006), *The Battle of the Sun* (2009) and *The Lion, the Unicorn, and Me* (2009). She also writes for screen and radio, and has a contract with *The Times*. Awarded an OBE in 2006, Jeanette Winterson lives in Gloucestershire and London. Website: *www.jeanettewinterson.com*

'For though we cannot make our sun
Stand still, yet we will make him run'
Andrew Marvell, *To His Coy Mistress*

THERE ARE SOME DAYS when the sun is so bright that when you look away everything turns black. I had a dog like that; a sun-black dog with the light in him so bright that the rest of life went into shadow when he was killed.

Now you know the end of the story but not the beginning, and the end of a story is, well, only the end, and much happens on the way there, like people who set out at dawn and sleep at nightfall, and the sun makes his journey with them.

So I will tell you how I came to find the sun running beside me, and how that brief and lit-up time has changed the way I think about things – not just the big things but the small things too, because, you will notice, the sun lights up everything – old socks, discarded magazines, dust, cobwebs, as well as the handsome house and the beautiful view. The sun will dazzle off a piece of broken glass as easily as off a church window at midday.

The sun is a democrat. Rich and poor alike stand in his rays. Dogs are democrats too, and don't discriminate between Gucci and worn-out. That is not to say that they have no discrimination – they do, but dogs are on the side of love. They love life and they love you, and they will valiantly do their best to love life, however inadequate that life may be, and they will valiantly do their best to love you, however inadequate you may be. Dogs are love on four legs. 'Yes,' they say, 'I will, and yes, and yes.'

I discovered that life could be *yes* instead of *no*. I discovered that life could be love and not its lack.

That's a big thing. Along with it I discovered that an old shoe is better than a diamond bracelet, and that a ball is the round world in little. When I threw him his blue ball he chased it as though it were the globe itself he was chasing through the wide heavens, eager to land the one place where life could be found. He brought it back to me, delicate, between his jaws, and dropped it at my feet, the world in little. Trust.

Happiness. Throw it again, and again, and again, make the world new, every day, and to him it was new every day, the sun rising on a planet still damp from its making, the clean, early air of a fresh start.

I had need of a fresh start.

What I mean to say is that sometimes something quite unexpected enters your life – something you did not plan for, were not even-if-at-all thinking about. I never wanted a dog. Dog was not on my wish-list or even my tick-list. I didn't notice dogs in the street in the way that boys notice cars or men notice blondes. I like animals but my life was not dog-shaped. My girlfriend wanted a dog, and I said yes because that was easier than a baby. The dog was a kind of *Jungle Book* baby, no schools or night feeds, nothing that couldn't be managed with a ball and a lead. Simple, easy, yes.

Yes, I said, I will, and yes, and yes …
So the dog came home.

Home. Home is so familiar that it needs no looking at, no explanation. Come through the door and home is just there. The pictures, the books, the kitchen table, the leaky tap, the sitting room painted the not quite right shade, and if there are things to do, well, they don't have to be done now. Sit down, have a drink, eat some supper, put the washing in the basket …

The dog took the washing out of the basket and ran with it like he'd found the meaning of life. Give those trousers to me! *No!* Give them to me! *No!* Come on drop, good doggie … *No!* Holy Law of the Jaw: Don't let go …

He was called Maximilian on his pedigree. A King of Bohemia or some far-flung shore where miracles happen. I could have changed his name to Rex or Sam, but he walked like a Max; part-swagger part-comedy turn, and something of where the wild things are.

It was the wild thing in myself that he tamed.

It was my job to train the dog. He took it upon himself to tame me.

I have never settled. I have never said *yes* to someone else without reservation. I am not sure that I have said *yes* to life without reservation, as if by reserving something to myself, I would not be mangled, tangled, strangled by the demands of this world and the demands of others. It is not wise to give unreservedly. I am a generous person, kind and seeing, would withhold nothing except what must be withheld. There are gifts, and they are gladly given, but the self is a gift with reservation.

Absurd to love a dog so much that there was no reservation.

But I did.

When he was a puppy he went everywhere in a cotton bag. We took him to the cinema one night, and he slept on my knee all the way through the film and I pretended not to notice that my legs were getting wetter and wetter as his bladder emptied while he slept.

We took him to a photographic exhibition – still in his bag – and while we walked from photo to photo he stayed quite still, warm and soft through the bag, like a living secret, but whenever we stopped to admire something in particular, his curious black head popped out, and looked sleepily at the photograph, and sleepily at us, as if to say, 'You walk and I'll dream.'

And that's how it was when he was small, falling over his own feet, tiring and needing to be carried, us walking, walking, him dreaming, dreaming, a black curled-up ball of dreaming, a dream dog.

And then later, bigger, stronger, he did all the walking, me panting to keep up, never could walk him to exhaustion, his long strong body sleeking through the air like a thought that comes back and back, like a boomerang, flung out of sight but coming back and back. Out we went, long walks, long days, and then I was the one doing the dreaming, the rhythm of him releasing my mind.

I dream we will always be together.

I dream we will always be here.

I dream we are in a wood – a dark wood, and midway through it, midway through life. I dream I am travelling. The branches are dark with their own shadows. The crows are flying home. Night is falling. Black air thick with crows' wings. My black dog. It's late. Dream me home.

I woke up to the telephone. It's the dead of night. Where are you?

Do you believe that love is as strong as death? Not stronger, as strong as, the hostile twins fighting it out through the stretch of the universe. Who wins? Death takes the easy victory every time, but love never steps out of the ring. You want to fight? Fight this – you live in my life – not in my memory, not in thoughts – in my life, the cellular me, the renewing DNA, I am a part of all I have met, you are what

I met. Apart, yes we are, death can do that. Separate, no, love holds you there. While I am alive, so are you, we go on together because we can't be any other way.

And I think it's you, just up ahead, waiting for me. Always just up ahead now, waiting for me. I'll be there. You ran faster than I could follow.

I used to send him to stay with a friend in the country. She had a terrible time of it because he didn't understand that a hen is best left unmurdered.

She walked him long and hard, and he built sinew and muscle and muddied her kitchen floor, and when she took his bed away from the Aga, he dragged it back, and lay looking at her with his big eyes. He knew where he wanted to be.

It was the summer and every night she played him the BBC Proms on the radio and cooked her supper with the back door open and he ran in and out and her cats sat on the corrugated roof of the shed, their fur in ripples like the waves of the roof. And on rainy July-August nights she lit a tinker's fire with fallen wood and the dog and the cats sat in front of it, like different stars in the same sky. Animal-dark, animal-fire.

She said, 'He startled three deer, and chased them, amazed by their easy grace and light speed, and he tried to bound as they bounded, one, two, three, leap, one, two, three, leap, but they cleared the hedge and vanished like mist, and he was left, on his hind legs, puzzled, barking. *What kind of an animal vanishes?'*

She said, 'We crossed a fox, burning red, early, alone in the field, dew-heavy up to his belly in thick grass. Max gave chase, and the fox turned at bay, and threw all his red power at the black young dog. I wish you had seen him run, spine contracted, head down, blurring his paws to get away, and up the hill he came towards me, and stood panting, tongue out, looking back at whatever it was that had reddened him into flight. *What kind of an animal is red?'*

She showed him the world – the green world, the blue world, the white world, the river world, where he sprung in, flung in, chasing ducks, and scrambling out as joyful as every river-drop shook from him, racing the narrow muddy path, happy, happy. *What kind of an animal is happy?*

This one, this one, this one, this one, this one, this one …

I'm curled up now, narrow muzzle on my forepaws, drying off, fed, watching you. The whole world, look what we've got, the whole world.

Yes is chaos. *No* is control. Every yes I ever said brought with it a downpour, an avalanche, a heavens opening chaos and doused me in life, water of life, swept off my feet, better swim for it, deep breath.

He loved water. He was a spaniel. I loved the splendid chaos of him. My fearless dog, in chase, in repose, spinning universe of nose and paws.

Call him and he'll come. Call him.

He ate poison, twice, but it didn't kill him. He raced across an open road and a white van took him down. We waited all night, waiting waiting, he was so strong, but this time he didn't come back. I called and I called but he didn't come back.

Love is not one thing, one kind. Love is not one shape, one name. Love is chaos because it is bigger than any of the boxes it comes in, and as soon as you get it home, it fills the whole house.

He was so tiny the day that we brought him home; he grew, and so did love.

He stole my shoes, my cardigans, my pens, my gardening gloves, my string, my car keys, my heart. In return he gave me the sun.

Running, running, running, running, running.

Afterword

DAWN, BUT ONLY JUST. That magic time when there are no shadows. When the ragged edges of a hundred bamboo huts, and the harsh realities of rural living, are softened. When friends and neighbours are just waking: unaware, unprepared.

The arrival of the soldiers is a fist to the face. They come out of nowhere: on the backs of camels, in four-by-fours. Engines revving, hooves pounding, guns firing. Anyone who strays outside is shot where they stand – frozen in shock and fear before they fall.

Crops and houses are torched. The fire spreads eagerly, burning through the bamboo with arrogant ease. There is nothing left to do but run. Through the chaos, to the forest's edge. Don't stop. Don't look back. That place – that life – no longer exists. When you finally stop, the urge to vomit is overwhelming. You let it happen. You don't cry. Not yet. You need to stay strong, keep moving.

This is Muna's story. We have changed her name, but nothing else. Muna lives in Darfur, one of the poorest and most isolated regions of Sudan. It is in this vast drought-ridden place that, for the past five years, conflict between government and rebel groups has devastated the lives of millions of innocent civilians.

Oxfam is working with the hundreds of thousands of traumatised people that have been forced to flee to neighbouring Chad. Many like Muna are living in overcrowded camps. Many more remain in their villages, praying that each raid on their homes will be the last. Armed groups regularly and indiscriminately destroy or steal everything that is useful: crops, animals, water-pumps, even cooking pots. Until there is nothing left to take, except lives.

The camps are safer than the villages. Just. And it is this need for protection that has added an extra layer to Oxfam's work. From supplying clean water, to replacing stolen animals and basic household items, we now ask ourselves: 'How can we ensure that people are not at risk from violence?'

And not just in Chad, but in other countries around the world where conflict has turned ordinary lives upside down. Working in such dangerous environments is one of our greatest challenges. There are no magic wands. No big wins. But the little things, the details, can count for a lot. And in our day-to-day work we have found some small but innovative ways of helping people to protect their lives and their livelihoods.

A mountain of soap: giant oblong bars of candy-pink, ready for distribution. A huddle of donkeys – all female – patiently waiting to go to their new homes. Not obvious safety measures, but they are definitely helping to keep women, especially, safe from attack. Oxfam's soap distribution has meant that women no longer have to make so many potentially dangerous journeys to distant markets for what they need. And the female donkeys?

They can carry as much wood and water as the males. But they're not worth as much, so are less likely to be looted.

These are just two examples of how Oxfam is trying to ensure the safety of the people we are supporting. Each country, each context, is different. But the thinking, the plans, the activities, the consultation, the assessment of what's working and what to do next, are all there. In conflict situations worldwide, the protection of civilians is uppermost in our minds, and at the heart of our response.

The reasons why conflict is rife, in so many poor countries, are complex and varied. But one thing is clear. Peace cannot come without a plan to tackle poverty. Poverty cannot be beaten without peace. Conflict resolution is a tough nut to crack, but with patience, the promise of a more secure and sustainable living, and some passionate campaigning, it can be done.

Across West Africa, guns that have been surrendered through an Oxfam-funded scheme are being converted into tools and farming equipment. Community radio talk shows are encouraging their listeners to solve disputes without the use of violence. Training centres are offering new skills to young people – giving them the chance to earn a regular income and self-respect and, crucially, keep them away from guns. It's early days, but after decades of conflict across the region this is a giant step towards permanent peace.

Worldwide, around 1,000 people die every day as a result of armed violence. Many thousands more are displaced, maimed, or left traumatised and destitute. Much of the violence occurs in regions of the world that are already poor and where situations are already volatile. Weapons, affordable, available and easy to use, repeatedly find their way into the wrong hands – because there is little to stop them. There is no doubt that the unregulated arms trade fuels conflict and keeps people poor.

Oxfam has been calling for tougher arms controls since 2003. We have prodded, pushed and petitioned world leaders to close the gaping loopholes in the laws that govern the arms trade. And it is working. In December 2006, after three years of tireless campaigning, the UN General Assembly agreed to begin work on a historic, legally binding international Arms Trade Treaty. So far, so good. But the details are still being hammered out – by hundreds of countries. Resolve could wobble, heels could drag. In films, even on the news, guns are at a distance. In our living rooms, but, thankfully for most of us, not in our lives. For people like Muna, guns are a daily reality. Oxfam will continue to campaign for arms control until the ink has well and truly dried on a watertight international treaty.

oxfam.org.uk/controlarms